All Over

All Over

Stories by Roy Kesey

DZANC
BOOKS

All Over

Invunche y voladora

1. Llamas

As they wake in their rented cabin on the first day of their honeymoon in Chile, they realize, first the wife and then the husband, that they remember nothing of the wedding or reception. Neither mentions this to the other. The fire in the woodstove is dead, the cabin is very cold, and there are a dozen llamas gathered outside. No one told the spouses there would be llamas here.

The llamas, their delicate necks, their long lashes, their great soft eyes—they stare in through the massive bay windows as the spouses shower and dress, make breakfast and eat. The spouses prepare to leave, and the llamas mass in some sort of spiraling formation. The spouses step out the door, and the llamas attack.

Does the wife scream out? Does she panic in any way? She does not. The husband screams slightly, however. The spouses take up thick sticks of firewood from the rack by the door, they wield their firewood mightily, and slowly they drive the spiraling, spitting, biting beasts away, bleeding about the face and head, the llamas and spouses, all of them bleeding. Later the cabin manager will apologize for the incident. It must have been something they ate, she will say.

2. Fishing

The spouses' guidebook says that Chile has some of the finest trout streams in the world, but the spouses do not go fishing. They do not know how to fish and are not anxious to learn. They drive over many, many streams on their way to other places, and occasionally stop to take pictures.

As they drive, the husband begins to remember. The wedding is still blurred, but the reception line afterward comes clearer: the hundreds each with glass in hand, the congratulations and thanks, the many old women in old fur coats—or was it only one old woman, one old fur coat, and she passed through the line many times?

3. History

He is American, she is Peruvian; her eyes are onyx and his are shale. Three months ago she was pregnant, and both were thrilled and terrified. In eleven furious weeks they planned everything: wedding, reception, honeymoon. Then her blood came, and not just her blood. At the hospital the bleeding was stopped and the news was given: the child was gone. And the fiancée had been damaged, somehow. Not only not now, then, but never. The wedding was six days away.

4. Skiing

- Take me back to the lodge.
- You can't quit now.
- Yes I can. Take me back to the lodge.
- Honey, we—
- I'm cold and I'm tired and I want to go back to the lodge.
- I'm not taking you back to the lodge.
- Yes you are.
- No I'm not.
- Fine, I'll go by myself.
- You can't.
- Yes I can.
- No you can't. You don't know how to take off your skis.
- Take me back right now.
- No.
- I hate you.
- I know. I don't care. You can't just quit.

5. The Lake

After only a moment or two of staring at a lake beneath an overcast sky, one begins to see the dark shapes. Each time one looks away they rise up and slap down on the surface, creating unnatural wakes.

All day long as the spouses nurse their bruises, the lake is scarified by low wind, and the dark shapes writhe. The cabin manager tells the spouses that the shapes must be large fish or cloud shadows.

6. Puerto Varas

The spouses pack their bags and load them into their rental car and drive two hours farther south, to another cabin with bay windows and a woodstove. There is another, much bigger lake. And there is a volcano, or so the spouses have been told, but the volcano, the volcano out the massive windows, the volcano across the lake, it is invisible: there is not enough light to see.

The spouses wake on their first morning in the new cabin, and still the volcano is invisible, obscured now by clouds. This lake, too, is scarified by low wind, and the dark shapes rise and fall.

- Well, says the husband.

The wife nods, yawns, stretches beautifully, curls into him, goes back to sleep.

The husband stares out at the lake.

7. Horseback

As they wait for the guide to saddle the horses, little by little the husband remembers still more. She came in on her father's arm, and the statuary trembled; painted figures looked, and were amazed. Her father was in full dress uniform, long sword bright at his side, and the almost-husband wished that he had a sword too. But it didn't matter. She came to him all the same.

Now they are on horseback, it is raining and he is petrified. This was his idea, was supposed to be amusing, but the horses have been rested long and well on high pasture: they want to run. The husband had no idea that this was how it is, the tremendous speed through thick trees, the branches that reach for him. Every so often the guide catches up to him, rips the reins from his hands and leans back. The horses stop simply. But when the husband tries the same trick, his horse runs still faster, the wind and rain, he is numb and slipping from the saddle as the guide saves him yet again.

They ford a river, the water fast at the withers, and then they are climbing and the horses must walk. Above them hawks circle, and the husband remembers, "The Blue Danube" over and over, and he danced with his wife, her mother, his mother, her grandmother, his sister, her aunt, another of her aunts, still another, "The Blue Danube" endlessly, spinning and spinning and spinning like these hawks.

The rain has stopped. There are striations of sun through the varying grays.

- Look, says the guide.

They turn and look. The river is silent five hundred yards below them. The far lake is a gem of ten thousand facets. But even from here the volcano cannot be seen, is still cloud-shrouded and blind.

They take a different trail back to the stable, and the horses are content to walk, fern and pine and berry. The husband reaches out, takes the wife's hand as they amble downward. The spouses smile though their bottoms are very sore.

The husband tenses, there is a new smell, acrid and musky, and then his horse bolts. He clenches his legs to the horse's sides, hauls back on the reins but the horse gathers speed into trees, over snags and deadfall, into a clearing and there is an old wooden bridge, the husband drops the reins, wraps his fists in the horse's mane and prays as they're onto the bridge and it slants to one side, the river and rocks beneath them, the far end of the bridge, one piling is loose, the bridge wavers and shakes and they jump, the horse stretches out, they make the far side and the husband tumbles heavy into ferns.

He lies there on his back. Most parts of him ache, but nothing drastically, nothing in a fractured way. He stares up through bracken. The guide arrives, and the wife, breathless.

- What the hell was that? asks the husband as he gets to his feet.

- The urine of the puma, says the guide. It makes the horses afraid.

- Oh. Well.

- That bridge is a so dangerous place. You should have crossed through the water as we did before.

- All I did was hang on.

- This is not a ride for the beginners. Why did you say me that you are expert?

The husband glares at the bracken. Then he turns to face his wife. To his surprise her eyes are bright. Perhaps she saw how he jumped, how he cleared the broken bridge, how he flew. She smiles and now he knows: she saw.

8. Salmon

The ache, the pain, the tiredness: all this can be overcome. Other things cannot, and still the spouses try. Miracles happen, they believe, or there would not be a word for them. They hope. That is their one bulwark in this world. Despite the doctor's words, they believe it is not an impossible thing. They can hope. They have that right.

Today they go to a lodge with thermal baths, and a restaurant said to be the best in southern Chile. They spend hours in the baths, massaging one another's aches. They talk of the wedding reception, and each memory feeds the next. The marvelous marbled hotel, though the hall itself was low-ceilinged and unattractively carpeted. The tables, the flowers, the guests all glorious. The band members in tuxedos on stage, the long sweep of truffles, and the cake.

The cake! They forgot to cut their cake!

They laugh, and groan at their aches, and laugh, and thank each other for the good massage. Yes, they forgot to cut the cake, but perhaps it was cut later, by others, after the husband and wife had left.

And the food, how delicious the food must have been, the food they took so long in choosing, the food so splendidly arrayed, the food neither spouse had time to taste. The five wines he picked, the Pinot Noir, oh yes, and the fine hors d'oeuvres she selected, the prosciutto and stuffed artichoke hearts, all of it gone now forever, but delicious, it must have been delicious.

The spouses withdraw from the baths, towel one another dry, dress and proceed to the restaurant. The salmon cuts are massive and select. The wine is right. The lighting is subdued, the waiters attentive, the mousse precise. Things look good for another try.

Back in the cabin the wife goes to shower and the husband builds a fire. The pyramid of twigs, the single match, the thicker twigs, still thicker, and the thinnest of split branches. He stretches, pours two glasses of wine, adds more branches and a small log. It is an outstanding fire.

The shower sounds have ended, and there are other sounds now. Guttural gurgling sounds. He knocks on the bathroom door.

- Give me a minute, says the wife.
- Are you okay?

- Not really. I think the salmon—

More guttural gurgling sounds. The husband opens the door, steps in, is hit by the smell but staggers on. He rubs her back as she rids herself of the last of the salmon. She rinses her mouth and he rubs in small circles. He takes her to bed and returns to clean, the grayish orange everywhere, the specks of garlic and oregano, he wipes it all away.

9. The Day of Rest

The husband reads his Darwin, the notebooks from the voyage to this very region, and stares out the bay windows at where the volcano must be. The dark shapes turn and roil and heave beneath the surface of the lake.

And the wife in bed remembers other things. The night of their wedding coincided with the birthdays of five of their guests, and the five men gathered at the reception and were sung to. It was improbable and fine, and the voices rang out in that low-ceilinged hall, the band joined in and the toasts were dignified and sure. Then as they left, husband and wife, arm in arm, the cake forgotten and uncut, as they made for the door the guests began to applaud, louder and louder, the applause rose and swirled around them, as if they had done a marvelous thing, and they had, oh they had.

10. Yogurt

- You always do that.
- Do what?
- You never think about anyone but yourself.
- What are you talking about?
- How many yogurts did you just put in the basket?
- Three, I think.
- And all of them for you.
- I—
- What flavor are they?
- Um. Vanilla.
- I can't believe you would do that.
- Why are you making such a—
- You know I don't like vanilla.
- Yes, okay, but couldn't you just—
- Of course I could. That's not the point.

11. Farther South

She now understands how it will be. When the act is done, when they fall flushed and smiling to their respective sides, the hope lasts only a few seconds more. Soon it will not last even as long as the act; then they will give in, and it will be gone. She turns to him, and he closes his eyes. She puts her hand on his chest, and he puts his hand over hers, and does not open his eyes.

They pack their bags again and drive still farther south, toward the island called Chiloé. On this day at last the sun comes fully out, the lake glints and no dark shapes appear. On the far shore stands the white-tipped volcano, not quite as tall or jagged as the spouses had imagined.

The roads are lined with eucalyptus, and in every field are the bandurrias, long-necked and duck-sized and many-colored; they keen and take flight as the spouses drive past. She teaches him the *Padre Nuestro*, and he teaches her "The Star-Spangled Banner." Hours pass easily.

To Puerto Montt, and then to Pargua where the ferry waits. The spouses drive into the maw, park, climb to the upper deck and stand in the whipping wind. The clouds over Chiloé are dark but the air above the channel is clear. The island is a distant low bank of green. The ferry eases away, swarmed by seabirds.

At the dock in Chacao, the spouses drive out the far side as the rain begins, lightly now but thickening. They take a wrong turn, end up in a cul-de-sac, and there is a church. The church is closed. Beside it is a sign: Kilometer o. So it is from here that one might begin.

On the road to Ancud the spouses keep watch for the invunche, Guardian of the Cave, a coarse-haired monster fed on human flesh, head spun half a turn on its neck, one hand sewn into the muscled back—the spouses have done their homework, read their Chatwin. But they see no such thing, and are slightly disappointed.

Slowly the rain thins over acres of conifers and bare hardwoods. The hills are green, and the guidebook tells the spouses to be reminded of Ireland, a place they've never been. Along the highway that rises and falls are solid walls of hedge flecked with small yellow flowers, and men ripping into the walls with chainsaws. The men are red-cheeked but dark-skinned, short and strong and weathered. The spouses stop to ask.

17

The painter thanked them for their input, walked out to the parking lots and keyed their cars. He then grew old very quickly—constipation, osteoarthritis, pigmentary glaucoma. He could no longer paint, could no longer weld or roof, could barely plumb. This then was it: his one large bit of art was what there was to be, his sole source of sustenance if he was to be sustained, and now an idea, a final idea, an unpleasant but only remaining option.

No local driver wanted the load—too heavy, they said, uninsured, they said, no way I want no hairy-leg riding along, they said—so he called the Tulsa pay phone every twenty minutes for eleven days, at last got the trucker and they worked to agreement. Fifty-one hours later the rig arrived, mud on the flaps, dust on the dashboard, the trucker strung on meth and smiling. They loaded up, and with scrolling posts included they were no longer inside the GVWR, but the trucker twitched twice, cocked his head, said they'd give it a go all the same.

They skirted the scales, paralleled the mountains, tried lake-towns and failed. They tried river-towns, and failed there too. They tried everywhere else and at last fell into luck: Thrombaccus had aged but not died, was sick of its sickened view and would have them. Ten days, then, and nearly as planned, a kiosk raised, the questions of grommets and bearings and gears answered, the posts installed five hundred yards apart between the town and its mountains sullied by quarries and clear-cuts and roads.

It was one a.m. when they started the pull, the trucker up high and the painter down low, flashlights in their mouths as they walked the edge of the painting toward the far post; it was six a.m. when they finished, the dawn sky opening behind them, the edge now secured, just the two men and the vast stretch of paint, light and darkness, cornices and crags. They stood and looked. They nodded and shook their heads.

- Nice little picture you got here, said the trucker.
- Thank you.
- Still and all. Shame it had to come to this.

The painter agreed, but was fairly sure there were worse things. He paid the trucker, tipped him a case of Snickers, waved as the rig pulled away and now people were coming to look. He stepped into the kiosk. He took up his bullhorn. He breathed deeply once and began to chant, A Dollar a Turn For a Chance to Paint on a Painting!

The good people of Thrombaccus would mainly paint

more quarries, more clear-cuts, more roads, he knew, except for the children who'd perhaps paint giraffes; there would also be screeds and sermons, ads and aphorisms, Fuck You! and Asswipe! and Greta Please Come Home! When the current stretch was fully marred and they wanted their old new old view back, he'd run the scroll and they could start again. So it would go and the canvas would outlast his body; too bad, yes, but sustaining, and still a single thing, and as the line begins to form he imagines the postcard he'll one day send to Tulsa: All is well. Blue is kindness and grays are greed, but you already knew that. Keep her clean, is what I'm saying.

Cheese

"Redeemed and thus liberated."
- Carlo Ginzburg, *The Cheese and the Worms*

*I*t would appear that in the previous interrogation you contradicted yourself in regard to the provenance of the angels. Therefore clarify this circumstance and your belief.

Back to that again, are we? Once more: earth and air and water and fire were mixed together, and out of that bulk a mass was formed, the way cheese forms in milk. Worms appeared in the mass, and those worms, once blessed by God with will, intellect and memory, were the angels.

As if out of cheese, then.

So to speak.

Are we talking the whole celestial hierarchy here, or—

No. Archangels, and angels properly speaking.

Whence then the others? The principalities and powers?

As if out of butter.

The virtues, dominions and thrones?

Out of yogurt.

The cherubim? The seraphim?

Whipped cream and meringue, respectively.

I will have you know that meringue is not a dairy product.

Is that my problem?

Not your biggest one.

Which is?

That the Holy Roman Office of the Inquisition has charged you with twisting maliciously, with affirming diabolically, with contriving wickedly, with persevering obdurately, with causing to resurface and asserting as true the ancient philosopher's censured opinion that there was an eternal chaos from which originated everything of this world, and with resurrecting the Manichean doctrine of the dual generation of good and evil, thereby putting at risk the entire Counter-Reformation program as such.

All on account of the meringue?

Hardly. You—

Because I'd be willing to reconsider as far as the meringue goes.

You know perfectly well that meringue is but the beginning, and may I remind you that should said charges be judged true, you would be obliged to abjure your heresies publicly, to fulfill various unpleasant salutary penances, and to spend the rest of your life in prison wearing nothing but a habitello. Does that sound like a laughing matter to you?

The habitello sounds a little funny.

It is, a little.

Right. Next question?

Have you any knowledge of the future?

A tiny bit. Minimal. More sort of a presentiment than anything else.

Namely?

That it ends badly.

Badly is hardly the word.

Really?

I'm so very sorry.

Me too.

I cannot, however, allow my sorrow to change things.

Of course not.

I have a job to perform.

Yes, yes of course.

Don't think this is easy for me.

I would never think such a thing.

Because—

It's okay. I understand. Go ahead, ask the next question.

Right. Sorry, I just... Okay. Who are your accomplices? Your disciples? Your hangers-on?

You're kidding.

No, really.

Um. Counting Melchiorre Gerbas?

Melchiorre the Moron?

The very same.

Poor bastard. No, we'll deal with him later. Right now we're more interested in movers, shakers, folks that could be dangerous if your ideas took hold.

In that case, none that I know of. Pretty much everyone here in the greater Friuli area thinks I'm kind of a ding dong, religion-wise.

And yet there's no way a simple miller such as yourself could have come up with all these ideas.

There were the books.

Right, the books. Let's see, Boccaccio, Mandeville, the Bible, *Il Fioretto*... Nope, no dice, still too many loose ends. Names and addresses of everybody you've ever spoken with, if you'd be so kind.

You know I can't tell you.

And you know what happens if you don't.

Torture?

Bull's-eye.

I... Damn. Sorry, no can do.

Fine. Take that!

Ow! Never!

And that!

Ow! Never!

And that!

Ow! Francesco Montareale!

Okay, I think that about does it for now.

What's that supposed to mean?

That you will indeed be condemned as a heretic and heresiarch, and will be obliged to recite your abjuration, candle in hand, at the entrance to the cathedral; that during your two years here in this dark dank prison you will pray often, fast on Fridays, and seem most truly repentant; that in a letter to Fra Evangelista Paleo you will recant, beg forgiveness and mercy, and promise never again to fall into error; that you will gain a hearing, and at said hearing will weep and plead and prostrate yourself; that you will then be released, and resume to a certain extent your place in the community; and that at some later point you will start spreading your filthy lies yet again, will again be arrested and tried, will be condemned as a recidivist, and at the age of sixty-seven, on the direct order of Pope Clement VII, will be led to and burned at the stake.

Really?

That's what it says here.

Let's have a look.

See?

Wow. Well, if that's what it says...

Yes.

Hold on. According to this, I don't get tortured until my second trial, fifteen years from now.

We've tried to follow the spirit of the thing rather than the letter.

But you're getting the essentials?

Each and every one.

Good. Good good good.

So.

You're saying this is it?

Pretty much. See you in 1599?

No, hold on, don't, don't go just yet.

Yes?

And afterwards?

Afterwards when?

Once I'm gone for good.

Yes?

Does anything come of it?

You mean does anything come of your ideas and suffering and ignominious, horrifying death?

Yes.

Depends on what you mean by 'anything.'

Look, I'm begging you here, if—

Okay. I mean, I'm not supposed to, but, well, okay. Yes, something comes of it. After it's done, after you're gone, there will be a rumor, third-hand at best, that a peasant here in the Friuli has been heard saying that when the body dies, the soul dies too.

That's it? One lousy theosophical descendent?

Sorry.

Well. What's his name?

Marco, or Marcato. The record won't be clear.

And what becomes of him?

Nothing, as far as we know.

No uprising, no revolution...

Nope.

How depressing.

Yes. But there's something else as well. This book itself.

What about it?

Well... Posterity. Those who come later will want to know certain things, and this book will tell them, and without you there would be no book.

Things like what?

Like the manner in which one might use discrepancies attributable neither to suggestive questioning nor to torture between my questions and your replies to expose the filter that you inter-posed unconsciously between yourself and the texts you've read, said filter presupposing an oral culture composed partly of autono-mous but obscure peasant mythologies that might well serve as evidence of a millenarian cosmological tradition, said mythologies having later been grafted onto a complex of ideas ranging from a naturalism that tended toward the scientific to utopian aspirations of social reform.

Interesting.

Very. Also, and I'm sure you'll agree this is a good thing, it will hypothesize meaningfully in regard to reciprocal influences between the dominant classes on one hand and the subordinate classes on the other, and will use your very case, lacking in macro-historical significance such as it is, and representative by virtue of that lack, to demonstrate the extent to which one might exercise one's conditional liberty within the not altogether inflexible cage formed of the latent possibilities of a peasant culture otherwise known only through fragmentary, distorted documents from the very archives of those who sought to repress said culture.

Um.

I know, I know.

Will anyone read this book?

Mostly historians and their students.

Not promising.

No, but there will be others. A few others. A handful.

Enough?

For what?

Fair question. Although...

What?

I was just thinking. Maybe there's some way around all this.

A way to beat the book?

Exactly.

None that I know of. You could always try, of course. But bear in mind what you'd be risking.

Marco, or Marcato.

And the existence of the text itself.

Damn.

Yup.

So.

So.

I guess you'd better be off, then.
I guess so.
Take care.
You too.
Write when you can.
I will if you will.
You know I will.
And you know *I* will.
Okay then.
Okay.

Strike

*T*he black limos blurred in the shuddering cries and Mayor Tyrus strode tall, the glint of his tie-pin bright in the eyes of the millions. His garnet voice surged from Broadway to Third, "This is ours, thus are we, this is what we have built with our hands! World Trade and Citicorp! Empire State and Madison Square! Whitney and Frick and Guggenheim! Elsewhere in the world there is naught such as this, there are none such as us, and the gods themselves mumble and scrape! Let them come, let them barter and beg, let them measure themselves by our mink and minutiae! Manhattan!"

Dust clouded and broke and walls palsied, the millions rolled in those words and sang them back, all but you and I, Chantal, all but you and I—for to whom do such unholstered shibboleths belong? To Tyrus, his coral cufflinks, his jasper-handled jackknife? We leaned like elms and wondered what would come of the sum of such saying as the words bounced in shout from the beryl of Bleecker to the sapphire of St. Patrick's to the torrid topaz of Times Square.

You and I, Chantal, we slept in cardboard and dined on skinks and sowbugs. Do you remember our earlier days, here in the folds of the Ramble? Hubcaps for plates and milk-crate chairs, newspaper napkins and burlap smocks, but we loved in the old way, Chantal, we lived as we knew to live and love. Each morning you traced the horizon and scattered flecks of sunlight through the din; each twilight you quickened the weary woods and closed the flowers by hand. Our afternoon travels may well have been sorry and slim as at best we etched our path to the bank of the Harlem River, but in that slag we laid back to follow the play of gaunt arabesques from the smokestacks across the hoarse water, and there too was love, love as we had found and called it, love that limned our supple lives.

Then at the words of Tyrus something slipped; we dwelt restless in the dim hum of damp days, and chorused for the wounded sky at dawn. His echoed thoughts milled locust-thick in all the talk around us, while you and I waited husky and brown, waiting only for whatever would come, wondering if it could or should, and Chantal, at last it did: the garbagemen struck.

From our benched outpost in Washington Square we watched as they marched in their orange-clad ranks, their bright canvas gloves, their hats shifting cranium-white as they clashed lids like cymbals and hoisted their brooms and chanted in uniformed unison. They marched and we watched and behind us the chess players scythed: the knights' insidious splits and the bishops' sharp conniving, squat rooks nodding protection to pawns as royalty looked wanly on.

For a week there was only the dense old noise, the hardened breath, the wristwork and wailing lost in what fewer knew than had known before, a seldom sign bequeathing thinner good. What is the half-life of time, Chantal, and where should we go to claim it? We sat at the crux of street and lane, the silver and glassware streaming past, the balm and embroidery, white wool and spices and silk; to soothe the hours as they brindled by we invented impossible pets and told of their upkeep and feeding, we threw pots of dirt and spittle as we waited again and vaguely richer now.

For a week and more there was no further note of the strike, but there was a sense of it, Chantal, a swelling and strain, the brownstones choked with pie-tins and peels, with pheasant gnawed, promises kept, thoughts thought and smells smelled and sighs sighed. And what good was all this to us? What gathered in basements, on stairwells, it was all not ours but theirs, and would only be ours when tossed and strewn, for that was the treaty, however unsigned.

Which is not to say we ate worse than before: the city dumpsters were a turgid bounty. The strike stretched out and the dumpsters flashed, blue and green and rigid in the sun, there were rows of them and files as well, at last legions, and slowly they filled. And when they were full, the third week or fourth, the fourth you would say, very well; in the fourth week at last the citizens spoke, from Admiral Dewey Esplanade to the far reaches of Dyckman, from Franklin Delano Roosevelt Drive to the Henry Hudson Parkway. We hummed to the hymns of their bitching as we picked through the myriad piles: the dumpsters and basements and stairwells had filled, still the garbagemen struck, and now at last there were bags, every plaza and square, good lord there were bags, and though these were tied and twined against our strivings, the barons and dukes of the kingdom of dogs came to aid us, the dobernards and labrahounds, the fruit and frolic of a thousand streety nights— as are you and I, Chantal, as are you and I. The bags however tied and twined were no more than slow sport for the colliherds and boxeghans, the shreds like angel ash drawn high above the steam-grates, and when just enough became plenty we were welcomed and groomed and feted and sated and stretched.

The strike leaned forward into its second month, there were few bags and fewer and none, the garbage now dumped from windows and slung from garages, loose and brave and clever in the fog. The news was no longer for napkins, Chantal, but was play-thing and rune and chanson: vision and revision, foretelling and recounting, a north for you that was not me, a polestar for me that was not you, unimaginable game. And the magazines! The pictures! In the pictures were men in green with grenades, all squinting, all sweating, and lined against the garbagemen! This was a past and future to be feared or cheered, and we did, we cheered and feared and built our fill as the garbage mounted around us. The days of cardboard shivered and went, and home was a castle of plywood, Chantal, we lounged on painted plywood thrones, and dined on carrots and casseroles from the polychrome unwanted. There were refuse streams from each door to the street, trash hilled in the cul-de-sacs and mountained in the alleys. The sun set often and well on our domain as the lanes were mulched with coffee grounds, sprouted sofas, the eggshell-millipedes curled and writhed, a tale for each invisible leg and we smirked at the housewife slather and business bog, the napkins of the fast-food fey in all their marbled want.

Then the marches! The citizens! Who is to blame, they wished to know, and what has been done and what has been un-done, that things are not now as they once were? The citizens wove in the streets among their waste, held signs and banners, and we waved to them as we looted their lots, we waved and wished them well. Who is to blame, came the refrain, the Inspector General or Governor, the State Assembly, old Tyrus himself? Ah, but we had no answers, we had no questions, we had only all that was to be had, all that had been used and left and still the trash piles grew: tectonics of fractured sheetrock, pillars of balding carpet, and as the copyright crones and software sheiks ran tripwires before their doors, built machine-gun nests in parabolic antennae, the strike endured and we roamed and gathered, tonged and trifled, scavenged and salvaged and scrubbed.

And the speeches! First the appointed, Planning and Finance and Public Works, each director, each spackled explanation and how quickly they were shouted down, strung up, and spiked to the labyrinth walls! And then the archaeologists came, of the time before the strike they spoke, and were heeded by no one. But yes, but yes, they said: there were epochs, whole epochs when streets were clean, when we swept our walks and driveways, when we troweled and spritzed in ecstasy—there was nothing, you see, such as we see here, the hillocks of fishmeal and cornstarch, the swamps of salad and syrup, the tundra of torn roofing and the taiga of worn upholstery. The archaeologists spoke, and the people cried, But this, but this, we already knew, and whatever good is a truth so true that nothing remains to be said? The truths and their bearers were caught up by the mass, were borne to the shoals of shelving and scree, were impaled on picket and pole and left to hang.

Then the poets! Who would have guessed that the poets had so much to give, but from their lofts and attics they brought all that had gone thin. Their adverbs they hung from the streetlamps, and conjunctions fell like confetti; into the gutters and gaps they pitched their nouns and verbs, and we took them, Chantal, the ones we could carry, the several still breathing as best we could tell, we stroked their clammy foreheads and spoke of better days, we crooked them to our throats, we whistled our sinuous madrigal, and more than a few of them flourished in the hot rich manure of our souls.

When the poets were empty the artists came, old colorists and older chiaroscurists, encomiasticists and infantesimalists, aleatoricists and atavists and even appropriationists, and they begged us all to wear new eyes. On their backs they bore painting and sculpture, the message for once unconfoundable, for once it was instantly effable: this is the city in its final transmutation! The living portrait of our heavy bones! The only potent collage of our time! Add, add to this last mask, not in sorrow but in ravenous joy, sowing all that you have!

And Chantal, the painting was heard, the sculpture was heeded, though no one knew how or why: the citizens gathered all that they had and made homage there and were artists themselves for the first and last time. Therapists threw psyches from flowered balconies, typists hurled their gossip and mugs, accountants flung debits and loans, and the piles grew, Chantal, how they grew.

The blacksmiths and bouncers and bagmen took umbrage at what still stood; they slivered the walls and subwalls, the perpends and cornices, the keystones and columns and jambs. Slowly the skyscrapers faltered, over-ripe and splitting at the sides, but there was no rising of dust or girdered roar: the refuse wreathes held whatever fell, much as each jagged winter you'd held me, frost thick in your hair and the hurtling wind a death in every limb.

The moment of murmuring came just then as we all beheld what had been had and splintered. How to define the pigeons as they minced the sky, the bondsmen as they bowed, the tremulous hands of the hawker? Where is it written and who has transcribed the pacing and lilt, the tenor and tense of what stirred in the mouths of the many? Still we held back, you and I, Chantal, for there was something more to be had, and it was not at all clear who would have it.

Then came the first phase of migration, the gleaming Explorers and Scouts gunning up and into the waste, churning toward bridges and tunnels, but only the quickest and rightest slipped through, the rest caught and held in their rush, the vans and sedans and compacts and coupes unmoving and fine and idling and dead and abandoned: on each throttled street they were beautifully left to adorn what had fallen before, strings of colored metal like Christmas in the garbage eaves, citizens climbing out and each helping the next through the unsure footing of vinyl and shad, thrilled at the thread of their stark and sublime survival.

Second and short was the subway attempt, East 86th, Seventh and Houston, Union and Soho and Duarte Squares; at every opening into the ground a tremendous trying and failing, for the trains were now plinths in cathedrals of dross underground, the tracks long since packed with icons and clogs, with rainspouts and rags, with signposts and serum and sod. Back into the air came the masses, no choice but to walk and walk they did, the tunnels and bridges for some but for most it was north to what once had been the Harlem: if even before it might have been crossed leaping ice chest to life vest to buoy, the river was now a thoroughfare, a solid ground of divans and duff, of liver and logs, Manhattan no longer an island, unthinkable thought. Should we as well have walked as you wished? But how to know if the star ascends or the world only turns? And so at my word we stayed.

When the rest were gone the city became a suddenly si-

lent space. For minutes or months, Chantal, the stillness held trea-
sure, tiaras of thought, we tossed doubts like diamonds between
us. The absence of sound was a presence that pressed and sealed,
rose swollen and lush and damaged and healed, it lit and enfolded
us like cotton or old love. Why hadn't we been told of that amni-
otic hush and the ways it has of licking the rust from our eyelids?
Was there no one who knew, or no one willing to tell?

The silence lasted little longer than it took to be perceived,
dark Berkeleian mirror that it was: the city was ours and then no
longer ours as the dogs that had once been our allies lifted in their
blood, came in throngs from Ward's Island where they had bed-
ded down, crossed the footbridge to challenge our rites and rights,
our passage and goods, and bade us leave the kingdom of their
east. Besieged and besmirched we ceded ground, blended west,
but from Riverside Park came the empire of rats: their sacred text
had forecast the strike in all its detail and glory, and their chirring
scratched at the walls of our sleep as they poured through the acres
of waste.

We hoped for war, of course, a limpid slaughter to both
sides. The rats marched in full color to the concrete skirts of the
Met where the dogs were waiting, but there rats and dogs spoke
and signaled, signed and shook and split the city between them,
and we were betwixt and bloody, Chantal, we were baffled and staggered and holt.

There were days of slit panic, of pursuit and ratcheted
breath; we lobbied and clamored, shied and stammered, hailed and
hoarded and hid. At last, sewered and scarified, you held my wrist
in both your hands and asked the date of my death, the site of my
grave, and if I could be brought back. Had I any answer but what
I gave? You kissed my shoulders and flipped our coin; that coin
gave us west and we two bobbed and countered, we circumscribed
the peaks of siding and stovepipe, we fashioned dirks and scimi-
tars and stalked the papered valleys. The guardian rats were fat as
capybara and oh how we hunted, you with your trident of finest tin
and I with my lasso, my croquet bolas, my deep inimitable call. We
severed and slashed, stabbed and skulled, we stripped the finest
pelts away and sewed doublets and capes and leggings. We tracked
their herds and the emperor fell, the empress and all her court, the
burghers and merchants one by one, whiskers scant as we left them
and only the thinnest were spared as future serfs.

The dogs came to us then and saw what we'd done, they

quite literally impossible to locate, but then, that wouldn't be such a problem, would it?

   - No, I guess not. One last thing—do you, there at the *Instituto de Perfeccionamiento*, do you speak, in general, English?

   - We are speaking English now, sir, you and I.

   - Right, but the others, the, um, doctors or therapists or—

   - *Perfeccionadores.* Perfectioners.

   - Exactly, the perfectioners, do they speak English as well?

   - All consultations are—

   - Yes, yes I know. Well. Very well.

✍

He went. He left his house and got in his car and drove. He turned left, and turned left again, and turned right, and went straight ahead. He turned left and right and left and left and left, and then he hit the *avenida*. He'd never seen it before, but there it was. He turned right and drove up the *avenida* until it dead-ended at the bay. There was a white fence or railing along the cliff-top, and a fine view: the bay, the seagulls, the sailboats. For a time he stared at the view. Then he got back in his car and drove down the *avenida* until it dead-ended at a white fence or railing along a cliff-top overlooking the open ocean. There was a view here as well. Again the seagulls and sailboats, though fewer of both than before. After staring at this new yet familiar view for a time, he got back in his car and drove back up the *avenida*, and just as he was about to turn right into the maze toward home, there on the corner he saw a sign. *Instituto de Perfeccionamiento*, it said.

He parked his car and walked to the door, knocked and opened and entered. Inside was a small lobby or vestibule and to one side was a desk and behind the desk was a woman. She had large dark eyes and creamy skin and short dark hair and a pretty smile.

   - Yes? she said.

   - Good afternoon. You, we, I called earlier and we spoke, you and I, I believe.

   - Yes, sir, we did. One hundred dollars, please.

   - But—

   - Each session costs one hundred dollars, sir, regardless or irregardless, both are acceptable now, of the treatment received.

   - But—

He waited for her to interrupt him, and she did not.

- But... isn't that a little, I don't know, irregular? I haven't even seen the perfectionists yet. How do I know—

- *Perfeccionadores*, sir. Perfectioners. Not perfectionists, not in any sense of the word. 'Perfectionist,' sir, while likewise from 'perfection,' from the Middle English *perfeccioun*, from the Old French *perfection*, from the Latin *perfectio, perfectus*, was first used in or around 1846 to refer to or as signifier for an adherent to the ethical doctrine which states that the perfection of moral character constitutes man's highest good, or alternately b: an adherent to the theological doctrine that a state of freedom from sin is attainable on earth, or alternately 2: anyone disposed to regard anything short of perfection as unacceptable. Perfectioners are something else entirely, and no one ever sees them.

- Oh.

- I believe we will start with your skin.

- My skin? But madam, my skin... Well, okay, but it's not what I had in mind.

- Rest assured, sir, it's all part of the program, the program that has been chosen on your behalf. For now, try not to worry about the other aspects, the aspects that you did in fact have in mind. Those will be attended to in due time, insofar as they yield to our treatment—all of them, each and every one, insofar as they yield to our treatment, but in accordance with the program, and in due time. Now. Cash, check, or credit card?

He paid in cash and was shown by the large-eyed dark-eyed creamy-skinned short-haired dark-haired prettily smiling woman into a square waiting room. He sat down in the only chair, and the woman left, closing the door behind her too quickly for him to catch more than a glimpse of her splendid, better than splendid, quite genuinely ideal rump.

The walls were lined with bookshelves lined with books. After fifteen or twenty minutes of waiting he began to walk around, not in circles but in squares with sharp right angles, inspecting the books. None of them were in English. He wished he had paid more attention to his Spanish teacher in high school, just on general principles, just for the good of the thing, as none of the books were in Spanish either. After fifteen or twenty minutes of walking around in squares he sat down. After fifteen or twenty minutes of sitting he got up again and went to the door of the waiting room. There, he listened. He heard nothing. After five or seven minutes of hearing nothing he opened the door and walked out to the lobby or vestibule. Now there was no one sitting behind the desk. He waited at the desk for nine or eighteen minutes, standing rigidly though not at attention. If there had been a bell or buzzer of any kind, he would have rung or buzzed it. He called out. He shouted. He screamed. At last he rapped his knuckles firmly on the desktop. Then he walked out the door and down the walk and to his parking spot, got into his car, and drove the long drive home.

- What a gyp, he thought.

*

First thing the next morning, he stopped sleeping and awoke. He opened his eyes and stretched, closed his eyes and opened them again. He stretched again. He got up and went to the bathroom and turned on the light and removed his underpants and turned on the shower and looked in the mirror.

His skin was perfect.

It was blemishless.

His acne, the acne that had plagued him, a forty-year plague, the very acne that had served as Elizabeth Wannaker's excuse for not accompanying him to the junior prom, and she'd said it out loud and to his face and in the presence of many persons, his friends and hers, though mostly hers as his lurked a short distance away, It's those zits, Stanley, those zits, do something about those zits and then maybe I'll accompany you to a prom, though not the junior prom as it will be too late for that and anyways I'm hoping Harold Plansky will ask me. Do you know him? His friends? His phone number?

That self-same acne was gone.

As were his scars. The thin curvilinear pink line across the top of his left big toe from that time he'd dropped the paint-can, and god alone knows why he'd been painting barefoot, freshening up the trim around the front door like his dad had told him to, and what a weird accident, the can had caught him just right, opened his toe down to the bone, and paint everywhere, blood-colored paint, no way to tell what was injury and what was home improvement and his whole foot hurt like a bitch—that thin curvilinear pink line was gone.

And the purple gouge in his left shin from that time he'd been running through the shopping center and had turned mid-flight to see if the bikers were still chasing him and had smacked into the low stone planter—that purplish gouge, filled in and touched up, the same color as the rest of his shin, shin-colored.

And the slight pucker in his glans from that mucked-up circumcision—vanished.

And the jagged slash down his right cheek from that time his ex-wife had come at him with the bread-knife, not that he blamed her, he'd been heavy on the sauce back then and heavy with his hands—invisible as if undone.

And the horrendous molten rippling of his left cheek and ear and part of his scalp from that time he'd gone into the JC Penney's, the whole place on fire, stacks of outerwear and racks of innerwear blazing torch-like, to save the Billingham kid trapped and cowering in the dressing room, who ended up dying anyway the following year, mowed down in a crosswalk by an unknown motorist who did not stop and was never apprehended—all that horrendous molten rippling now baby-smooth.

And the five mauve nickel-sized welts scattered irregularly across his chest from that time when RT Pickaxe had run into a whole goddamn battalion of NVA maybe ten clicks into Cambodia, unable to hold the LZ and god was it hot, the perimeter brought in tight, calling for air support, calling for extraction, and he heard a voice, the voice of Johnson, and Johnson said the chopper was delayed but air support would be there in zero-six, would lay it down thick and close and give them a chance; three minutes later there was no one to return incoming fire but Stanley and Rahlan Drot, the rest of the team KIA and broken, and Rahlan Drot, the one Montagnard left who'd been with him from the start, Rahlan Drot with a shattered femur, the gooks closing in, and Stanley had taken Rahlan Drot on his back and oh how he'd run, the brush ripping at his face and the air keening sick all around, he'd hit a trail and no choice now, up the trail he ran, three gooks in front of him and reaching but he put them down, and how he ran, he dodged them all, all but one, a short skinny dude with an SKS carbine, and the bullets opened holes across the front of Stanley's shirt, five holes, black-rimmed and loose-fringed, and he'd dropped Rahlan Drot and fallen, and old Rahlan Drot, good old Rahlan Drot had taken Stanley's CAR-15 and waxed that short skinny gook, had picked Stanley up, an unbelievable thing, Rahlan Drot losing blood, the shattered femur, but he carried Stanley to the secondary LZ that Johnson's voice guided them towards, they'd popped smoke, purple and yellow and red, and the chopper had come, had pulled them out, by god an unbelievable thing—those five mauve nickel-sized welts, they had been polished away.

And what had become of Rahlan Drot? Stanley stood staring into the mirror in his bathroom, the light on, the shower running, his underpants balled in the corner. Had Rahlan Drot made it through to the end? They'd kept in touch for a time, but then the letters had stopped. Plenty of reasons why that might have happened, though. Say he made it. Say he is even now an aging man, a smiling happy aging man, the shattered femur healed not by any *Instituto de Perfeccionamiento* but by time and the body itself, the marvelous body, and Rahlan Drot with his wife, a tiny woman she must be, tiny and lovely and kind, and the two of them tend small fields of rice, and at times in the evening their children and grandchildren come, walking the long walk up and along the ridge, the grandchildren laughing and playing and at times oddly cruel, but only in childish ways, and Rahlan Drot rests in his thatched and stilted longhouse, chats with his wife and his children, watches his grandchildren play.

Stanley stared into the mirror, stared at his perfect skin, and an old word came to him, an old and funny and appropriate word, a word his mother had often used back when the two of them were still speaking, and he smiled, and stared at himself in the mirror, and said the word:

- Gadzooks! he said, perhaps from 'God's hooks,' swearing by the Crucifixion nails, archaic, used as a mild oath.

Or perhaps Rahlan Drot hadn't made it.

❧

On Sunday he returned to the institute, and the institute was closed.

❧

On Monday he returned to the institute, and the institute was open, and behind the desk sat the large-eyed dark-eyed creamy-skinned short-haired dark-haired prettily smiling woman.

- Hello, she said.
- Hello, he said.
- Are you pleased? she asked.

   - It is a miracle, he answered. Or at the very least miracu-
lous. You even perfected my glans.

     - Not me, sir. The *perfeccionadores*.

     - Even so. A miracle, or at the very least miraculous.

     - We here at the *Instituto de Perfeccionamiento* aim to please.

     - But I don't understand. How—

     - You are not meant to understand, sir. You are meant only
to be pleased. And now, I believe, your hair. One hundred dollars,
please.

     - My hair?

     - Your hair.

     - But my hair, my hair, I like my hair. My hair is fine. Or if
it's not, and okay, let's say it's not, let's say it's graying, gone a bit
thin on top, but no big deal, no particularly big deal, nothing I can't
handle.

     - You're forgetting about the program.

     - Look, okay, the program, but if I want to fix my hair I can
just go to the hairdresser and get a damn haircut, can't I. And for a
damn sight less than a hundred dollars.

     - If that is what you wish, sir, by all means, you may. If what
you wish is to get your hair fixed, you can and may just go to the hairdresser and get a damn haircut. Do not let us stop you. We here at
the *Instituto de Perfeccionamiento* are neither interested in nor capable
of fixing things. If we fixed things, the institute would be called the
Instituto de Reparación. It is not. We are not. It, we, is, are the *Instituto
de Perfeccionamiento*.

     - Well, hell.

     - Yes, she said, from the Middle English, and that from the
Old English, akin to *helan*, 'to conceal,' the Latin *celare*, the Greek
kalyptein, compared metaphorically and perhaps also likened literally
to war by General W. T. Sherman. Have you come to a decision?

     Again he paid in cash, and again he was shown into the wait-
ing room. Again the chair and the sitting down, again only a glimpse
of the ideal rump. Again the bookshelves and books and the fifteen
or twenty minutes and the walking around and the sharp right angles and the inspection and the wish. Again the sitting, the getting
up, the walking to the door, the listening, the hearing of nothing,
the five or seven minutes, the opening of the door, the walking, the
lobby or vestibule. Again the nine or eighteen minutes, the lack of
bell or buzzer, the calling out, the shouting, the screaming, the firm
rapping of the knuckles, the opening and closing, the walking, the

long drive home.

⁊

He awoke in the morning with perfect hair. Movie-star hair. Thick and wavy and lustrous, unlike it had ever been. He did not have to open his eyes or stretch or get up or go to the bathroom or turn on the light or remove his underpants or turn on the shower or look in the mirror. He awoke and simply knew: he could feel its perfection against his scalp. He would never have to rinse or shampoo or condition ever again.

And so it went. Skin, hair, refrigerator, eyesight, wardrobe, gastrointestinal tract, sofa, car, unicycle, hearing, pogo-stick, flooring, plumbing, prostate, wiring, fingernails, and so on. Drive, walk, knock, open, enter, chat, pay, walk, sit, glimpse, wait, inspect, wish, sit, get up, walk, listen, hear, wait, open, walk, wait, stand, call out, shout, scream, rap, walk, drive, over and over.

Then she said, Your program, sir, is complete.

- What?

- Your program is complete.

- No, I don't, it can't be, I'm, we're just getting started, just getting going, just getting into the groove.

- No, sir, I'm afraid we're not doing any of those things. Your program is complete.

- Well, okay, but surely there are, there must be, aren't there other programs?

- Not for you, sir. I'm sorry.

- But— But what about my fear of heights? My fear of lows? My nightmares? My echolalia?

- Sir, you do not suffer from echolalia.

- But I can feel it coming on right now at this very moment! "Sir, you do not suffer from echolalia." You see?

- I'm sorry, sir. Your program, your only program, the one and only program for you, it is finished.

- But what about Rahlan Drot? I'd give anything just to know if he made it, and if he did, to get back in touch, to know that he's okay, doing well, being happy. And what about my mother? She's old, extremely old, ancient and kind-hearted and courageous but we haven't spoken in years—she's never forgiven me for allowing my ex-wife to get away. And my ex-wife, speaking of my ex-wife, beautiful woman, I don't blame her a bit for what happened, and she, well, yes, she remarried, but I heard she's since redivorced, so she's free now, reunattached, and there's nothing in the world I want more than to have her as my ex-ex-wife, to try again, to do right by her this time.

- I'm afraid that none of those things fall within our pur-view, sir. That is to say, none of those things yield to our treatment. Your program is complete.

- But—

Again she did not interrupt him. He sought a way to end his sentence. He found it nonendable.

- So I guess this is goodbye, he said.

- Yes, she said, an alteration of 'God be with you,' 1573, a concluding remark or gesture at parting; see also 'adios,' 1837, from the Spanish *adiós*, from *a*, from the Latin *ad*, and *Dios*, from the Latin *Deus*, used to express farewell.

Back to his car, his perfect car, back to his house, his per-fect house. He walked immortal in circles and squares, one perfect room, and then the next. He ran his fingertips across his perfect skin. He ran his hands through his perfect hair. He ran across his perfect carpeting, stumbled over his perfect roller-blades, slammed headlong into a perfect wall, and there was no mark upon it, no mark at all, and his head was also still perfect, no pain, no swelling, no blood, and he ran from his living room to his kitchen to his hall-way to his bedroom and the three pictures framed on his dresser: his mother, her apron stained, the rolling pin held up for show, the flour on her cheek, her laughter caught and held; and Rahlan Drot standing next to Stanley, the small brown man and the large white man, their arms interlocked, Rahlan Drot's earlobes pierced and stretched, Stanley's tigersuit faded but clean, this one moment permitted, friendship and trust, this one moment of grace before the next descent; and his ex-wife, the first day of their honeymoon in Cabo San Lucas, behind her the ocean stretched out calmly and bluely, the low white wall of the terrace, the orchid in her hair, he'd told her how beautiful she looked, he'd raised the camera and she'd smiled and averted her eyes.

At the Pizza Hut, the Girls Build Their Towers

*O*ne serving per customer is the salad-bar rule and so the girls build: round walls of peach and cucumber slices, brick by brick along the edge of each bowl and then up, ten and twelve inches high, beautiful in their way, the interlinked colors. The girls argue about whose tower is tallest, whose bricks are most perfectly aligned, and tell each other how great their new haircuts look. They watch the manager and the manager watches them; the manager starts to twitch and the girls pull out their cell phones and call their boyfriends and whine about that Jennifer bitch who's always hanging around, and they keep one eye on the manager, for their time is coming, and now it comes: the manager thinks Fuck it, it's only salad, and tells the assistant manager he's going on break, and heads out back for a cigarette, and the girls tell their boyfriends they have to go but okay maybe at Amber's house on Saturday because her folks are going out of town and she's got that huge Jacuzzi thingie in the bathroom. Then they hang up, and push four tables together, emplace their towers near the outermost corners and return to the salad bar with empty platters.

They build the curtain wall with its battened plinth, croutons for ashlar and Thousand Island mortar, and above they build battlements, the wall walk floored with potato sticks, pierced pine nuts inserted for arrow loops, the crenellated parapet with diced ham merlons corbelled out to allow for Seven-Up machicolations. They build a gatehouse of baked yams with gherkin drawbars, more croutons and this time Ranch mortar for the flanking towers and guard chamber, pasta salad spurs, and now the manager is back and bitching and they say Yes but we paid for it and it's all totally nasty now so it's not like anyone could eat it and leave us alone or call our lawyers if you want, whatever, but leave us alone you stupid dork.

They weave sprouts to form a portcullis, construct an iceberg lettuce drawbridge, add a barbican and four bartizans and then Amber calls and her parents aren't leaving after all but so okay and they call their boyfriends back and say How about up at the dam instead and Yes I'll remember the blankets this time and Don't invite Willy he's so annoying and Okay and I'll call you back in a minute. Other patrons are gathering now and the girls glare until they go away, and ignore the kitchen staff poking their heads out except that one cute one what's his name except he's got soap suds in his hair what a loser.

They pave the outer, middle and inner baileys with romaine and spinach, build a great hall of broccoli, a pantry and buttery and kitchen of feta, a garderobe of tortilla chips, a solar lined with purple cabbage. What else? A donjon! So a motte of grated carrot, pickle turrets buttressed with shredded cheddar, a mushroom mural chamber. Then the stables, stacked chicken breasts for the walls, egg troughs, artichoke mangers. And the chapel! They totally forgot the chapel! Chamfered bell peppers, a heart of palm steeple, toothpick transoms and mullions, a dried cranberry altar and half an olive for the piscina.

Awesome! Nothing left now but the moat, chick peas held together with blue cheese dressing and grated parmesan, the ditch filled with Coke, squeezed beets to get the color right and bacon bits for offal. And now some old guy comes up and says someone should call Guinness because this has to be some kind of world record in terms of castles made out of salad fixings, and the girls say Look you perv either you leave us alone or we're calling the cops, and after a moment he does. Then they begin to eat, and in twenty minutes there is nothing left, and that's totally okay because the girls are gorgeous and shall live forever.

Loess

-A few questions first, if I may.
  - And of course.
  - Fine, then. The goal?
  - There are two: the overthrow of this world, and the construction of the next.
  - Right. And what, may I ask, are your qualifications?
  - I have read the classics, farmed rice, kept accounting records. I was a soldier for six months. I applied and was accepted to police school, law school and soap-making school but did not attend. I went to business school for a month. There were other schools as well. Then I became a library assistant. During winter holidays I walked through the countryside, and took rain-baths when it rained. Also I have edited newspapers and organized certain organizations.
  - Outstanding.
  - Are you with me, then?
  - Entirely. Will we work together or in parallel?
  - For now you shall go and I shall stay, and in our respective places we shall organize still more organizations. Then you will return, and we will ally with our domestic enemy against the foreign invaders; I will help to plan uprisings for you and others to lead, and they will be wildly successful and then fail horribly as the alliance dissolves. You will be captured by our domestic enemy, and your execution order will be signed, and a former student of yours will help you to escape; I will also be captured, and my execution order will also be signed, and I too will escape, and hide in tall grass until nightfall, and slip away. Nearly all of the members of our organizations shall subsequently and quickly be slaughtered. Is that all right with you?
  - Perfectly. To work.

☙

It was not simple, but it was managed, that which has been mentioned, and other things: a flag was raised, and an army. Thought was remolded forcibly when necessary, and of course the domestic enemy began extermination campaigns. The foreign invaders took the northeast, and in the northwest there was famine, men and boys standing beside roads, their stomachs swollen with dirt and bark and sawdust, men and boys only as the women and girls had already died or been sold; men and boys standing naked having exchanged all possessions even clothing for food and they stood and the sun weighted their skin and they stood and their eyes closed and still they stood and then died: several million.

Extermination Campaigns One through Four were turned back, the defenders successfully melding elasticity and mobility, secrecy and ambush. During the Fifth Campaign, however, these requisites were mislaid; the domestic enemy routed and chased them, and executed their families, and likewise killed or else relocated all others who lived in areas under dispute, the short-haired and/or large-footed women all killed, and the long-haired, small-footed women made concubines, and the children called war orphans and sent as slaves or prostitutes to cities, and when a million more were dead it was time for another plan.

☙

- We cannot stay here any longer.
- And where will we go?
- Northwest, to the cradle.
- But our domestic enemy lies wholly between it and us.
- So we shall travel circuitously: six thousand miles of walking and fighting, walking and fighting.
- But most of us are shoeless!
- Unfortunately yes.
- Through twelve provinces...
- And over eighteen mountain ranges, and across twenty-four rivers.
- Walking and fighting and climbing and crossing without rest?
- Of three hundred and sixty-eight days we shall spend two hundred and fifty marching; we shall skirmish daily, and fight fifteen

major battles, but otherwise, yes, rest, though even that rest will be not rest but sharing, speaking with those through whose lands we walk and fight, and we shall need a way to convince them not only to join us but to lose their very them-ness and subsist in all five senses of the word in us-ness, not one-of-us-ness but us-ness itself...

    - Perhaps... Perhaps theater!

    - Theater! With messages!

    - Anti-foreign-invaders-and-domestic-enemies, for example.

    - And pro-us.

    - Superb, but we precede ourselves. The four lines of domestic enemy defensive works, their nine regiments, how will we—

    - Walking and fighting, walking and fighting. We shall march at night when possible; the wounded will be left behind with those few who can be spared to fight rearguard, two years or three, as long as they last, and any leaders caught then paraded naked in bamboo cages and beheaded. Once through, a feint south, then a push west to the first of the rivers, a doubling-back, a ploy, a quick battle, and we'll all be across in nine days.

    - What then of the Lolos?

    - We shall ally with them, and follow them on and through to the Tatu. The river will rise and swell and rage as we ferry much of our army across on three boats left stupidly unburned. There will be constant aerial strafing as of the third morning, and the domestic enemy will push hard towards us, and no choice then for those not yet across but west to the Bridge Fixed by Liu.

    - Liu!

    - Liu. Those already crossed shall fight and we shall race but the domestic enemy will arrive first, will remove all planking from our half of the bridge, will emplace machine guns.

    - And then?

    - The chains. Volunteers, hand over hand, and they shall mainly be annihilated, but one shall make it halfway across, shall then hang beneath and be protected by unremoved planking, shall throw grenades and shout terms of encouragement, the bridge will be ordered burned but too late, those already crossed will arrive and the enemy will run.

    - That is fortunate.

    - Very.

    - Then the highlands and mountains.

    - Yes, and here many more shall be lost to the cold, the fatigue, the precipices. But there will also be things worth taking from those with too much: ham and duck and salt.

- Duck!
- Precisely.
- But what of the Hsifan, and the tribal Mantzu?
- They shall roll boulders upon us, and we in turn shall steal and eat their wheat, their beets, their massive turnips. Many too will be lost to the swamps, and there will be no shelter from the rain, and there will be no fire to cook our food or warm our bodies, but the cradle will at last not be so distant.
- And having once arrived—
- After several more battles here undescribed—
- Where exactly will we live?
- In the caves.
- Cave-caves?
- Loess caves!
- Loess, of course, loess. But will there be enough of them?
- We shall not need so many by then.
- Heavy losses?
- Eighty percent.
- Disastrous.
- Disastrous indeed, but survivable.

ↄ

It was not simple, but it was managed, that which has been mentioned, and other things. The caves were temperate and dry, and soon were fitted with floors of stone, rice-paper windows and lacquered doors. The lower loess slopes fluted down towards fields of wheat, corn, millet; the hills themselves were twisted and scored by water and wind, and with the changing of the light became brigantines, ballrooms, battlements.

New preparations, then, and new organizations: the Young Vanguards, the Children's Brigades, the Elder Brother Society. Large-footed women cleared and planted; small-footed women pulled weeds and collected dung. And of course all that was owned by those who owned much was taken: goods, crops, land.

Old poisons were drained, and all doors replaced when soldiers left homes they had been lent. Mass justice took the form of executions. Factories were looted for necessary machinery; handbills dropped by the enemy giving bounty amounts for each leader were flipped and bound for schoolbooks.

The question, now, was time and how to fill it. Responses: classes on reading and writing, and political lectures, each student bringing his or her brick to answer the lack of chairs. There were public health and factory efficiency competitions. Clay models served as instructional aids for history and geography, strategy and tactics, anatomy and surgery. There were broadsheets giving praise, criticism and something a little like news. There was ping-pong. When military circumstances permitted there were group walks into the hills, gazelles and buzzards to watch, and hot water was drunk, and it was called white tea. There were card games, war songs sung to the music of old hymns, and of course always theater, needed greatly now as policies occasionally changed: in the first act of each play the old policies were followed and errors were thus committed and hundreds died theatrically; in the second act the new policies were followed and the result was triumphant marching.

Throughout all this there were small attacks on their base. Then the domestic enemy leader was seized by his own generals while organizing Extermination Campaign Number Six. He was not released until he'd agreed to desist, to ally, to attack the foreign invaders instead. The invaders however did not wait for the allies to arrive; they schemed at the Marco Polo Bridge, came in full and took half the country. Soon on other continents too there were millions on ships and in tanks and on foot dying, and the war here against the foreign invaders became part of that greater war, a war that took all the world. This greater war ended well, the invaders driven now wholly out, new bombs dropped by greater allies, the no-longer-invaders disappearing in smoke, their shadows burned into their concrete.

や

- And now?
- Another war.
- The domestic enemy again, yes. Will they be definitively defeated?
- It will take three years, but in the end the remnants will be driven to an island, and the remnants will pretend to be us, but they will not be us, and the world will be made to know.
- Peace, then.
- Yes.
- Stability at last.

- Also.

- The world overthrown, you and I together as before, all else below us and time for a construction of the new.

- Though for a project of that nature and size, perhaps we would do well to invite the participation of others.

- Others, yes, to make manifest that which we design. A Minister of Commerce! Of Education! Of Industry!

- These yes of course, but more importantly, no fewer than four hagiographers. And someone to rewrite all literature. And a former emperor to garden. Also...

- Yes?

- Also...

- Is something wrong?

- Also... Yes. Beyond the peace... It is as if I cannot see.

- I can.

- Can what?

- See beyond.

- But how?

- The gift, simply, has been given.

- And? How will it go?

- You shall begin well, abolishing the sales tax, the camel tax, the salt carrying tax, the salt consumption tax, and also the taxes on pigeons, middlemen, land, food, special food, additional land, coal, pelts, tobacco, wine, stamps, boats, irrigation, millstones, houses, wood, marriage and vegetables.

- Magnificent!

- But you will also have certain other ideas.

- Will they too provoke happiness?

- Those with differing ideas will be accused of mistakes of subjectivism, of economism, of reactionary and feudalistic atavisms; you will order them killed or imprisoned.

- Yes, but my ideas, will they provoke happiness?

- You shall stage your own foreign invasion of a nearby land filled with glaciers and temples and yaks so as to secure hydrological resources in perpetuity, infuriating actors and actresses everywhere.

- Their opinion is of no consequence.

- You will have the entire country making steel in their backyards.

- Steel is important!

- All other work will be abandoned; factories, schools and

hospitals will close, and the crops shall rot in the fields.

    - Oh.

    - In the following years, unfortunate droughts shall occur.

    - Ah.

    - Perhaps forty million will die.

    - That is a large number.

    - Immense, yes.

    - We have many to spare, however.

    - Spare?

    - And we can always tell everyone that it was nonetheless a success.

    - That is an option, yes.

    - And then?

    - Your power shall be reduced, and things shall be returned to how they were before your steel idea insofar as that is possible.

    - Unthinkable!

    - Yes, but true. However, you will subsequently recover much of the power you had lost.

    - Excellent.

    - Well...

    - What?

    - You shall apply all your remaining energy to designing and implementing a new system of primary education; soon enough the children will be very young adults who will praise you, and act vastly in your name.

    - They will perform great feats?

    - Feats, at any rate. They shall worship you, shall announce that all you say is true. You will disappear, then return, and employ them to destroy all who oppose you.

    - That sounds all right.

    - In a manner of speaking. Unfortunately you shall have additional ideas.

∾

It was not simple, but it was managed, that which has been mentioned. Also, other things. A play satirizing their leadership gave the necessary opening; gambits were played, counterattacks organized, tentacles extended.

The result: eleven million teenagers now held all practical power. Playing hooky pleased them, as did the establishment of tribunals and the meting out of punishment. Intellectuals were of course pilloried first. When there were no more intellectuals the teenagers went simply from house to house, even into their own houses, and brought their families forth. The chewing of broken glass was obligatory in certain circumstances, and of course millions died.

All who might at some point provide opposition were re-educated in labor camps. Classical musicians were made to play outdoors in the rain to keep sparrows from landing on branches; economists were made to catch cockroaches, and to count them; and all were made to make bricks, and paint asphalt streets, and dig large holes.

The teenagers smiled at the police and the army and bade them crawl. They set fire to libraries and museums, temples and mosques and churches. Any who did not now participate or cheerlead were likewise pilloried, or sent to the provinces to shovel manure, or obliged to write about the wrong things they liked, such as Mozart, that they might better be criticized for liking wrongly.

∾

- That was unfortunate.
- Yes, and it is not yet quite finished.
- Is there to be a future upside?
- You shall continue to be praised as a god for a time.
- All right then.
- Though in fact by this point you shall be only a figurehead.
- And who will hold true control? You?
- No. Others. I shall try to slow the worst of them. A coup will be attempted, but you will escape, will still have certain allies, and the coup leaders will be caught and disappeared. Later, other rivals will emerge; by then you will be mainly insensate in all three senses of the word, and I shall just barely defeat them, and the worst of it shall be over.
- And we rise again?
- No, we die. Me first, then you.
- But afterwards our works live on?
- For a time. Then they are repudiated. Then they are ignored. Then they are forgotten.
- Will we at least be remembered?

- Your body shall be preserved, though not much later every-one will wonder why. Our names, of course, our names will be remem-bered. Hundreds of millions of copies of your sayings will have been sold but will now be seldom read.

- And who will then lead?

- The man who shall establish the Two Whatevers.

- These whatevers, they will be successful?

- No. And he who established them shall not last long; curi-ously, the next man to lead will be one whom we regularly demoted and often discussed eradicating but never quite did.

- Will he lead well?

- In some respects, considering. He shall rehabilitate many in need, though nearly all those who thought will be gone irrevocably. After him there will be others. By then your sayings will be tourist curiosities. Those who destroyed in your name will be tried and im-prisoned and executed where practicable. Your mistakes will continue to be condemned. Martial law will be applied at times, and new pro-testors suppressed—in this at least things shall be consistent.

- I had hoped for better.

- I know.

- Ah, well.

- Indeed. There is always the further future, of course, though it cannot yet be seen.

- Onward, then.

- Onward, yes, onward.

Calisthenics

*T*here was a perfect rectangle and he walked outside, down the block, and now the restaurant. The restaurant girl, beautiful through the window. He did a jumping jack but she turned away.

Farther on a woman and she smacked him against a wall. The wall smelled terrific, cool and damp and cementy as he fell. He hit the ground, chipped a tooth, looked up at her huge against the sun.

A ride and some questions and painted bars for a while. Sweet sweet cement but his tooth hurt a lot. A guy offered him a thing and took him by the scruff of his neck. Then someone came for him. She said things and he nodded a lot. Most people were mostly right.

At home the person was still saying things and to make his tooth hurt less he imagined that it was an elephant. The restaurant girl, was she calling out to the cook? He hoped that she was and tomorrow he would find her and ask her.

Night. The television had things and he watched them. The restaurant girl would just now be getting home and still had grease on her hands, sweat on her face, he was sure of it. Time, time. The television things moved. She only wanted for him to be happy. He did a toe-touch, and then another.

Blazonry

1. Shield: Argent, three Garden Gnomes rampant Sable.

Monday evening and the package arrived at last, a magic package, anyone could see that. Who sends packages tied with string these days? No one, that's who, and the advertisement Wayne had torn out of the magazine in the checkout line months before had been very clear if only in one respect: total satisfaction guaranteed or your money back. It had seemed a good idea and still did, exactly the sort of thing to have on hand just in case.

Wayne snuffled, set the package on the sofa and observed: no return address, no indication of the contents. He nudged it to the left, back to the right, brought out and opened his pocketknife, traced lightly from corner to corner with the tip of the longest blade and knew it was not yet time.

e/ɔ

Nearly noon and his boss called him over, asked what had gotten into him.

- Nothing, said Wayne.
- So what the hell? said Jennings.
- I think I'm coming down with something.
- So go to the doctor.
- I think I might. I think I just might.
- Whatever, Wayne, but get on the stick a little, okay? I need you to be sharp. The company needs you to be sharp. It's a question of necessity at this point.
- I know.
- Do you? We've only got until Friday morning, and this is a big account. A huge account. We need this account, Wayne. You, me, the company, we all need it. Do I have to remind you of what happened last month? Of Simmons? Of White? Of Blanchard?

\- No.

\- So you show up after lunch girded for battle?

\- Girded, yes, absolutely.

\- Your hauberk, your helm, your halberd?

\- Totally and completely girded, yes sir.

\- Because unless we get this account—

\- I know. Believe me, I know.

\- Okay then. I'm not asking for miracles here. It isn't a question of miracles or magic or what have you. It's just a question of—

Jennings stared at Wayne; without looking down, he lined up his pencils, then his pens.

\- What's so funny, Wayne?

\- What?

\- Did I say something funny? There's nothing funny going on here. We need to be clear about that.

\- Got it.

\- Good.

Jennings lined up his markers, and Wayne nodded, headed back to his cubicle, not whistling but nearly.

∾

The newspaper was waiting on the porch. Wayne bent to pick it up, and there was a bark and a shout; he stood, shaded his eyes against the late sun, and looked over at the other half of the duplex as if he didn't already know who and what had shouted and barked.

\- You piss on my roses one more time, mister, and you'll be sorry as sorry gets!

His neighbor, Mrs. Dargo: early seventies, skin dry and scaly across her face, eyes too far apart, pet rottweiler built like a grizzly. There had been a time when he'd offered to help with her gardening and groceries, but she'd been yelling like this for weeks, and he wondered how much work it would take to get her committed.

\- Do you hear me? One more time! I dare you, mister! Pull out that slinky dick of yours just one more time and the Neighborhood Tenants Association will have your ass on a platter!

The dog whined, tugged at the leash, barked again. Wayne shook his head and went inside.

- No one's been urinating on your roses, Mrs. Dargo, except maybe your dog. Why don't you—

- I watched you, mister! I watched you walk right over and pull out that slimy wang of yours and whiz all over my Royal Edwards!

Her wind-up was comically slow, her release much quicker, and whatever it was she'd thrown caught him flush in the face. The smell was familiar and then he knew: he'd just been beaned by a muffin. He brushed the crumbs from his eyebrows and the blueberries from his hair, and she was gone.

3. Supporters: On either side a Great-Tailed Grackle proper holding in the beak a Wiffle Ball Argent.

Wayne opened the medicine cabinet, threw back a shot of cough syrup. There was a pinching sensation behind his eyes, and another low in his back. He eyed the bottle, swirled the syrup, drained it.

Back in the living room, the package on the sofa: curiosity swept him up, and he shook the package lightly. There was no sound. He shook it again, more firmly this time, and heard a tiny tinkling. Wayne set the package softly back in the cabinet, slammed the doors, locked them and tossed the key into an empty planter.

He headed to his desk, took up sheaves of paper and rearranged them, and rearranged them again, and rearranged them again.

෴

- Wayne. Wayne, Wayne, Wayne.

- Yes?

- I thought you were going to get on the stick.

- I was. I don't know what—

- I'll tell you. You've lost your edge. Remember that edge you used to have? Well, you've lost it.

- I'm doing the best I can.

- I know. I'm thinking that's the problem. Anyway. You know what happens now. I wish there was some way around it, Wayne, I really do. But there isn't.

- Maybe I could—

- If it makes you feel any better, it isn't just you. Miller, Ve-larde, Deschutes...

- But what if I—

- Nope. Out of the question. Sorry, Wayne, but you know how it is.

ༀ

Wayne waited until midnight. Then he waited until two. Then he waited until three thirty-five, filled the squirt gun with the last of the vodka, and dressed in the only black clothes he had—un-returned tuxedo pants from his brother's third wedding, silk disco shirt he'd been meaning to toss for years, dress socks and wingtips.

He stood on the porch feeling well and truly girded for once in his life. Who filled squirt guns with vodka these days? No one, that's who, though of course he wasn't really sure, perhaps many people did, perhaps everyone, everyone in the world. He put the barrel in his mouth and squeezed the trigger and drank until the gun was empty, then ran out into the rain and across the yard and urinated firmly on each scraggly rose.

Mrs. Drago's porch light went on, and Wayne caught parts of himself in his zipper. There was barking, and clawing at the door; Wayne limp-sprinted back across the yard and hunched into his house.

4. Motto: Fortuna bona, amicus!

A stormy Sunday morning, far-off thunder, hangover finally fading and time to observe more thoroughly. Wayne scrabbled in his desk, pulled out a magnifying glass, hobbled to the sofa; he cupped himself carefully, sat down and turned on the lamp.

There were creases in the heavy brown paper, and tiny stains, some of them squarish and dull black, some long and thin and gray, and some of shapes and colors that for unclear reasons made him think of gryphons and sprinklers. Wayne turned the package back and forth, took deft mental notes: on the bottom, the string was frayed as if the package had been dragged across rough surfaces; on the right, one large round portion of paper was slightly darker than the rest. A leak?

Wayne's cough rose and he hacked and sputtered. He stumbled to the bathroom, ransacked the cabinet, got half a glass of water down. He took his temperature and it was uncommonly high.

&

- She's dead.
- What?
- Mom's dead.
- She—
- I didn't know who to call, so I called the ambulance people. They should be here any minute.
- William... William, is this some kind of trick? Because if I drive all the way over there and—
- She's been dead a while, I think. All I did was go out for groceries, but then there was so much traffic, Wayne, and I tried but that intersection right there in front of the supermarket, all the honking and shouting, I tried but there was no way through.
- William, are you sure? Have you checked her breathing? Go get a little mirror and—
- Her breathing was the first thing I checked. Then her pulse. There's no breathing, Wayne, and no pulse, and she's blue and I've got to go, I can hear a siren and that's got to be them. Please come, Wayne. Please come as soon as you can.

Wayne listened to the dial tone for a time. It was almost certainly a ploy, but before he could think of a way to lay it bare, the doorbell rang, and Wayne flinched and winced.

&

An hour later and the package on the counter before him, his open knife in his hand. The NTA representative had been polite but intractable: he'd showed Wayne the footage from Mrs. Dargo's infra-red surveillance system, had said he was sure there were mitigating circumstances but that given the video they couldn't possibly be mitigating enough, so Wayne had until the end of the month to sell and move out.

The leak, if that's what it was, had gotten worse, the dark spot now ever so slightly darker. Wayne turned the package over. Again, faint tinkling. He slipped the blade under the string, closed his eyes and waited. Maybe it still wasn't time.

He opened his eyes, inclined the blade, the string stretching, stretching. But wasn't there even now a certain strength inside him, perhaps able to deal with headaches and backaches and a mangled scrotum, perhaps capable of handling both unemployment lines and duplex-hunting? He checked and there it was: a small but certain strength.

He closed the knife, put it in his pocket, set his hands on top of the package and exhaled. But what if his brother's call hadn't been a ploy? He took up the phone, dialed and listened: five rings, seven, nine. He hung up and dialed again, six rings, ten, fifteen, and now sweat crawled beneath his clothes.

He ran the package back to the cabinet, locked the doors, returned to the kitchen for his coat and car-keys. The vicious rain, his trusty Corcelle, he worked his body in and slammed the door, got the car started, backed down the driveway, stopped to wipe at the fogged-over mirror and the motor hiccoughed and died.

He turned the key back and forth and the motor caught again, lightning flared to his left and something exploded against the window to his right, a fury of barking and bared teeth and he hit the gas, spun into the street, was smacked and rolled and bundled.

Upside-down, Wayne waited. There was a vast pleasant numbness. There appeared to be no sound at all in the world. Then there was yelling, and the numbness faded, and he hurt in so many places. He crawled out a shattered window and got to his knees.

Mrs. Dargo smirked from her porch, the dog now silent beside her, and the pick-up driver was coming, waving his arms in rough oval glyphs. Wayne nodded, stood, wiped the blood from his eyes, pushed past, staggered up to his door and through. It was time now, no question, and where had he put the key?

He searched his pockets, the countertops, thought briefly of possible clues—meatloaf? rhododendron? okapi?—and ran for a hammer and screwdriver. He pounded at the hinges until the doors fell, and someone was yelling from his porch but now he had the package in his hands; he pulled out his knife and slashed at the string, at the paper, ripped open the box, removed two sticky bags of air, eased out the soggy contents and held them up to the light.

Fontanel

Yes, a separate collage for each and every birth; this one I finished just moments ago, a wealthy young couple from Chile. Now, look closely, the uppermost picture: this is the husband, who often does his best. Here he is packing a last few items into the wife's suitcase for their trip to Clínica las Condes, the finest hospital in Santiago.

Clockwise and spiraling inward, yes. Here is the wife, repacking the items correctly. She had not wanted a second child so soon, is looking forward to the end of this discomfort and weight. The baby at this point is eight days overdue but in no danger as far as anyone knows. The couple met with the obstetrician this morning, and he agreed to induce labor tomorrow, to perform a caesarean if necessary, but two hours ago at the hairdresser the wife felt the first twinge; her water broke in the taxi on the way home, and the contractions are now eleven minutes apart.

The couple's first child, fifteen months old, and of course the idea of a baby brother is unclear to her. She has however sensed the growing tension and throws food more often than before and strikes out at strangers and bites her parents when given the opportunity. The absolute lack of expression on her face is due to the fact that she is watching her mother, another contraction, the strongest yet, the pain and pressure deepening.

This is the wife's mother, with whom the couple's daughter will stay. Here she stands in the living room waiting to be asked to accompany them to the hospital instead.

This is the gas station attendant who is friendly and serviceable and pretends not to notice the wife's screams.

This is the drunk who swerves at the couple and misses.

This is the receptionist who assists the husband in filling out the paperwork, her gaze lifting only when the nurse wheels the wife away.

Here is the wife, changing into her gown in the labor room upstairs.

Here is the husband observing the receptionist as she turns toward the filing cabinet: her elegant neck, her slender waist, the smooth stretch of thigh exposed by the slit in her skirt, and he smiles as he remembers, then frowns.

This is the nurse administering the wife's enema. The nurse has been in love with the obstetrician for many years, would leave her husband in an instant if the obstetrician ever showed the slightest interest. The wife's expression is less a response to the warm water entering her colon than to her memory of the birth of her first child, and that first enema, only water coming out, and later the obstetrician, the look on his face, he had asked her for one last little push before heading to the delivery room, and she had complied, had sprayed him with feces, and that look, the tremendous disgust, how could he have let that look cross his face?

Here is the husband smoking out on the curb, squinting at the night, knowing his presence is not yet needed or desired and pleased at said knowledge.

Here is the wife as her pubic area is shaved. This too brings unpleasant memories of intense subsequent itching. The swabbing and sterilizing will have no such implications, however, will in fact be almost pleasurable. The nurse grimaces in response not to her work but to a thought of last night, her husband refusing yet again to accede to certain of her desires.

This is the obstetrician as he arrives. You should know that his jokes are never off-color, and that his hands are strong, a reassuring strength.

Here the husband holds the wife's hand as she begins another contraction. Note the empathy in the husband's eyes. Note the flower pattern of the comforter, and the strangely intense medium blue of the wall. All of these things are crucial.

Here is the taxi driver scrubbing the back seat of his taxi.

Here the wife is between contractions, and isn't her hair magnificent? That tube there is her IV; the other tubes are never explained, and the foot intruding into the frame from the left is that of the husband now dressed in scrubs and slumped in a hard brown chair.

This is the anesthesiologist, receiving news of the wife's dilation from the obstetrician. There are hundreds of anesthesiologists in Santiago, and of all of them this man is the best. His doses and pacing are flawless, his needle placement impeccable. He too is in love with the obstetrician, and also with the nurse, and they have no idea; in his free time, he works with small mammals in his basement.

Another contraction. Note the feigned empathy now in the husband's eyes; he is thinking not of his wife but of Marcelo Salas' hat-trick against Peru in a World Cup qualifier five years ago, and simply wants this thing to end. Note also the digital monitor there on the bedside stand. From up close the readout would look as if it were that of a seismograph, and of course in a sense it is.

This is after the epidural has been inserted but before the anesthetic has taken effect. Observe how strangely the wife and husband smile.

Here the wife is no longer in pain and awaits further dilation. She and the husband attempt to rest, and share last guesses as to whom the baby will most resemble, and agree for no good reason that the husband's father, recently deceased, is the most likely candidate. They of course make no reference to the fact that the baby might be anything but healthy and whole.

This gloved hand on the wife's distended belly is that of the nurse, and where is her other hand? Surely it is inside, prodding. On the wall behind the nurse hangs a bright metal-mesh box holding a number of blurry instruments, or is it one single blurry apparatus?

Here the husband stares down at the wife. The black object on the padded bench there behind him is unidentifiable.

The anesthesiologist, checking in to make sure that the epidural has not interfered with dilation. Of course it has not. He stares at the nurse. In a moment he will stare at the obstetrician. He has named mice after both of them.

Here is the wife looking up, though it is not known at whom, and these numbers on the monitor are likewise mysterious. 69.1 what? 41 what? As you see, the readout is now very long, the peaks ever higher, ever closer together, and where has the flowered comforter gone?

The wife's mother, carrying her whimpering granddaughter in large circles, begging her to fall asleep.

The receptionist, off work at last, alone in her apartment, staring out the window.

The wife again, her fists clenched, and yet she smiles as she is wheeled to the delivery room. It is to be assumed that her cervix is now dilated ten centimeters or very nearly so. I believe that the blurring of different parts of her body to different degrees is due to the irregular movement of the gurney.

The obstetrician, in love only with himself. It is a rich, consuming love, and beautiful in many ways.

The empty labor room, and now we see clearly the apparatus in the metal-mesh box on the strangely intense medium blue wall.

The hall, its almond trim, the wife still being wheeled toward the delivery room and smiling. The nurse pushing the gurney, note her eyes, her walkie-talkie, her hope that one day the set of thighs spread by the obstetrician will be her own, her wrists handcuffed to the bedrails, her feet lashed into the stirrups, the obstetrician in studded leather scrubs, a whip instead of forceps. Farther back the trim appears more pinkish than almond but if memory serves that

row morning, or if he will have to stop at the bank first.

The wife lying back, the IV line still in her wrist, her opposite hand hidden, and the husband staring at the pediatrician, who stares back, and grins, and wonders what must happen for love ever to be requited.

The family: the infant, one hand at his mouth, neither comfortable nor unhappy clutched as he is correctly in the wife's arms; the wife, her complicated smile, her face pale and swollen and exhausted, her hair somehow still beautiful, the thin twisting tube, her covered knees still spread; and the husband there with his mask pulled down, his wide, less-complicated smile nonetheless a stew of happiness and relief and love and pride and guilt. To the left, those gloved hands rubbing themselves together, they are not the obstetrician's hands. And that effect you see, the variegated blues of the wall, brightest in the center and darkening toward black at the edges as if the photograph showed an aura rippling like a pond into which a stone has been thrown, each successive ripple a darker ring—I have no explanation for that effect, no explanation whatsoever.

This is the gas station attendant in his bedroom in the house of his parents, masturbating to the memory of a glimpse through plate glass at the hairdresser as she reached for a comb days ago.

The wife crying as she touches the baby's face, a shot you yourself have seen many times, have perhaps even taken, and she cries because she has no idea who this person is; he is hers because they have handed him to her, and he is whole and healthy and it is over and has begun, but she knows nothing about him, and those are the husband's bare hands barely visible.

This small bright object in the nurse's palm is the needle that the obstetrician will use to sew up the wife's perineum. Do you see how curved it is? It is also very sharp.

The receptionist, removing a pen and a pad of paper from her nightstand.

The baby boy laid screaming in a plastic bassinet, and you see how clean he is though there is of course still a bit of blood and whitish foam in his hair. His coloring is good, his eyes swollen nearly shut, the camera's flash reflected in the plastic, the thick shadow above him no cause for alarm.

Similar but out of focus, the baby's body uncovered as if he had thrown the blanket off, though of course it is more likely that the nurse has drawn it back so that this very picture might be taken.

The gas station attendant's parents, watching television downstairs.

Again the baby, again out of focus, strong light shining in from behind—perhaps a reflection off the back plastic, perhaps something else altogether.

This is the vein in the inner wall of the wife's vagina as it is nicked by the curved needle making its penultimate stitch.

The father smiling at the baby whose testicles are a surprising red, and immense in proportion to the rest of him.

The baby yet again, back on the wife's chest for no clear reason.

Here the bassinet is wheeled out, the nurse looking over her shoulder as if something were perhaps being forgotten.

This is the blood pooling slowly inside of the wife.

And here at the center, yes, a collage-within-a-collage: the baby boy now wholly clean, wizened and screaming in his bassinet in the viewing room, his eyes ever so slightly open and their color indiscernible, his face distorted perhaps because the picture was taken through the plastic or perhaps because it is simply out of focus, and the other bassinets all empty; the wife resting in the recovery room, eyes closed, smiling, she feels no pain as yet, and as you see her robe has slipped open to show this one full and magnificent breast; the gas station attendant watching television downstairs now that his parents have gone to bed; the husband stretched out on the brown leatherette couch in the room to which his wife will soon be brought, his arm draped over his eyes; the anesthesiologist extracting a pygmy rice rat from its cage; the daughter waking suddenly, screaming; the obstetrician tying his shoes, whistling as he observes his own hands, the strength of them, the reassuring strength; the hairdresser asleep and dreaming of a gas station attendant glimpsed through plate glass as she reached for a comb days ago; the wife's mother, her head bowed; the husband's father still dead and decaying, the taxi driver still scrubbing but now at work on the carpet, the drunk laid out in the morgue; the nurse standing in the shadowed hallway, and the pediatrician alone in the break room twisting his cloth cap tighter and tighter in his fists; the receptionist in her lace nightgown, leaning back against the headboard of her bed as she chooses the perfect word to end a letter never to be sent.

Sheephead something something

So start it off with Sheephead something something (research but also the city aquarium, the display between the tanks, notes somewhere) also called sheepie/goat/fathead, live in kelp forests, wrap themselves in mucous cocoons to sleep, eat mussels squid urchins abalone, use their teeth to pry shells from rocks (how crush them? research). Something too about they sometimes, what was it, they sometimes are seen out of the water just hanging on to a mussel or something, hanging on with their teeth, the wave receding and the fish just hanging there, not letting go, something. Only spawn once a year. Young do not resemble adults—start off bright orange with spots, then dull pink, then finally like that bad old motherfucker in the big tank, black tail red body black head white jaw big old blood-colored eyes. Something about gorgonian something. The big thing though, the pay-off: they switch sexes at certain point during lifetime (precise term for this? hermaphrodite? proto-something hermaphrodite?), point being they're all females as young fish and males as old fish, point being the males are by definition always robbing the cradle, every old fish has to find a young fish, by definition a younger fish.

So.

So to make it work she'll need to be younger than him, stretched out on the bed naked et cetera or under the covers but naked and he'd wake her up but that would annoy her, everything he does annoys her these days and vice versa sometimes but he tries god how he tries because that's what you do, you try. Under her head then a pillow of some kind, a white pillow, off-white. On the nightstand (something about, they don't just change over out of the blue, but when the lead male dies the lead female becomes male? research) one of those magazines she reads that he hates but still sneaks a look at sometimes, and once he read that she could have twelve

10. Sorry, I'm not at liberty to comment on those years as such at this time. Suffice it to say, they are not "missing" as you so blithely assume. By no means are they missing.

11. Frankly, Datatechnocelucom has everything I'm looking for in a company. Not too big, not too small, fully integrated interface optimization, laser-stippled defragnifiers, cutting-edge seminars in six-star hotels on paradisiacal islands with hula girls and umbrella drinks and anonymous-bank-account facilities of all kinds, or so I'm told. And I've always wanted to live here in Chicago. The city is, well, you know what it is, it's got everything, you've got the museums, the pizza, the sporting events, the atria, the pizza...

12. Okay, fine. My family was, it was, let's just say my parents were typical. Absolutely typical. Perfectly average, is what I'm saying. The golden mean in every possible sense of the phrase.

13. Childhood, ditto. Your average town—everybody knows everybody, lots of small shops, decent schools, dying lumber mill, city council loaded with hoof-and-mouth activists.

14. The schools? Well, you know, your basic, I don't know, corndogs for lunch on Mondays and Thursdays, hamburgers on Tuesdays and Fridays, bag lunch on Wednesdays. Light beatings. Well-chaperoned playgrounds. Tetherball, jungle gym, Simon Says, soccer, foursquare, Smear the Queer, tag, softball, Cops and Robbers, dodgeball, Bugger the Misfit, kickball, Red Rover, basketball, duck-duck-goose, Cowboys and Indians, football, Sodomize the Outcast, red light green light, chicken-chicken-turkey... You know the drill.

15. Married, assuming that she survived somehow. If not, widowed.

16. In one sense, no, as we had no children. In another sense you are all my dependents.

17. Personal weaknesses, well, I'd say fudge. With walnuts. I'm crazy for that fudge with walnuts, hot out of the oven, and a glass of cold—

18. Oh. In that case, boy, hard question. Maybe, yes, a certain confidence that is sometimes mistaken for arrogance or conceit, but make no mistake, it's really only a certain confidence, so I guess that's not actually a weakness, is it. What else. I prefer that orders be given in a way that implies they're more sort of just suggestions, you know, something to keep in mind, something to perhaps experiment with, rather than something I have to do right this goddamn minute, goddamnit. Otherwise I occasionally react, not badly I'd say, but definitely not as calmly as some might wish. Some supervisors that is. There have been incidents.

19. And also, one other thing if you've got room for it there, the thing with the tears, the weeping.

20. I don't know how to explain it. I just weep. The tears come, and won't quit coming. No sobbing as such, no nose-blowing, no noise at all really so you don't have to—I'm saying it wouldn't be a case of other data processors getting up from their computers, interrupting their work, coming over to my cubicle to see what's wrong. Nothing like that. Just the tears themselves, salty and wet and eternal. Occasionally the ledgers themselves get a little damp, and when that happens, and I apologize in advance, but I've got plenty of experience with that kind of thing as you can well imagine—there are ways of drying them out such that it's impossible to know they've ever been damp, drying techniques that you personally can't even dream of.

21. Once, my wife's foot slid up and down my shin as we lay in bed. I was trying to write a poem in my head, but... Love or art? *Love or art?*

22. The answer is love, you moron. Art can always wait for later.

23. Above all, I think, a data processor has to be organized. Organized, and educated and qualified. Also he has to be experienced and capable, he or she, and easy to work with, and self-starting, and team-playerish.

24. In one word? Well, if I had to choose only one word, I guess that word would be 'peckish'.

25. Pretty much everywhere. The world over, in fact—over and over and over, believe you me. Aachen, Bydgoszcz, Cleveland, Dorking, Ephesus, Funchal, Gubbio, Hel, Iowa Falls, Jamnagar, Krk, Llandudno, Mamalamalama, Nanao, Odendaalsrus, Philippopolis, Qana, Ramalamalama, Sod's Bottom, Tallapoosa, Unye, Vyshniy Volochek, Wienerville, Xochimilco, Yuty, Zwolle... I'd continue, but you've quit listening.

26. Once again, I'm afraid I'm not at liberty to comment. Sorry, I'd like to help, but it's, I can't, sorry, just totally out of the question.

27. The best part, without a doubt, is the actual processing of the data. Just flat-out processing it, becoming one with the data, full speed ahead, blinders on, nothing but you and the ledger and the computer screen. And the worst part, probably I'd say the office picnics. I fucking hate office picnics. Mandatory attendance, forced merriment, boozy superiors, off-color comments during the three-legged race, sidelong glances behind the barbeque, cheap-ass mustard.... Fucking hate that whole scene.

28. I left because they did not recognize or appreciate my capabilities, did not reward me sufficiently for said capabilities, and gave no indication of any inclination to recognize, appreciate, or reward me sufficiently for said capabilities in the future. Also because of what happened with the mainframe.

29. Yup.

30. Long story.

31. Oh, really, it was nothing. One little explosion and everyone goes nuts.

32. What, other than the tiny faucets? Nothing special, except maybe the one where I'm flying over the countryside without an airplane, my arms outstretched, just me and the birds soaring above the clouds, the wind furling my long blond hair, and—

33. Yes, in the dream I always seem to have really long, really blond hair for some reason. What else. There's another one where I'm being pursued through the suburbs of Duluth by giant jellyfish,

and one where I'm writhing in the hellfire that no amount of water can extinguish, not even Holy Water fresh from the font, my skin blistering, my eyes melting and dribbling down my cheeks, and it goes on and on and on, the pain, the anguish never-ending. Your basic dreams.

34. Well, I once felt the thumb of absinthe pressing into my brain, but I don't believe it affected my job performance in any way or shape.

35. Or form, right.

36. None that I know of, except penicillin, chalk dust, mold, cigarette smoke, cashmere, liquid nitrogen, metal of any kind, plastic, wood and goat dander.

37. Yes. As Marcel Marceau famously remarked, " ".

38. Pet peeves as such, none really, except for how she always used to leave the toilet seat down. Drove me nuts. Or, if the question referred more to the workplace, as I think maybe it did, and you might as well have said so, then yes, several. When people steal your ideas, for example, or take credit for your projects, or put shards of glass in your lemonade. All of which is just basically disloyalty I guess, so, sure, pet peeve, disloyalty would be number one.

39. Another long story. We were sailing from Ramalamalama to Wienerville, and a big storm came up—waves thirty, forty feet high all around, wind at eighty knots. So we battened things down, the hatches and whatnot. I was on the tiller and she was on the sails, and I don't know exactly, to this day I can't really say for sure, but the mast snapped and the boat rolled, we both ended up in the water and I think she must have gotten tangled up in the ropes down below. I just hung on to the gunwales as best I could, hour after hour, and every so often I heard her voice—what I thought was her voice, though it could well have been something else, was most likely something else at that point, surely—telling me that everything would be all right. So I just hung on, and finally, after drifting for days and days and days, I got picked up by a freighter or battleship of some kind in the channel there between Tasmania and Boogooboogoo.

40. Right, sorry, lines, not ropes. You're right, yes. Lines.

41. Well, it's a very small island, more just sort of a big rock, really, but that's what it's called. And that's where I got the dingo, incidentally. They're all over the place down there.

42. For me the ideal working environment would be utter silence, utter calm. No coworkers, no boss, no subordinates. And no colors—the floor, the walls, the ceiling all a dull, soft white. Maybe one tiny window set in the door, but otherwise, nothing but white. And soft. Soft and white. Not totally unlike that room over there, in fact, unless looks deceive. Could I get a glass of water or a cup of coffee or something?

43. Great. And do you think you could... Ah, terrific, that's great, thanks very much.

44. HTML, too. Did I mention that?

45. Of course. Don't you?

46. Like the Mormon Tabernacle Choir would sound if all the choir members were fairies.

47. You know, fairies, small imaginary beings, gossamer wings, grant you three wishes, that sort of thing.

48. Nothing out of the ordinary. What to do, how to do it. I rarely listen until it gets to be too much, and even then it's only to shut them up. You know?

49. The only problems I've ever had involved mostly scapegoating of one kind or another. Nine jobs in a row, something goes wrong and I'm the scapegoat. I could fucking rip their hearts right out of their chests, I really could, especially that guy at that one place, Schellenbirder, something, whatever his name was. As far as bosses and/or supervisors go, no, nothing really, nothing I remember. As long as they give orders in the form of suggestions like I said, and keep their hands to themselves, you know, and aren't too stingy with the office supplies, the pens and pencils and paper and envelopes and letter openers and pens and scissors and paper clips and

staples and staplers and desk calendars and calculators and rolo-
dexes and pens and computers and printers and masking tape and
white-out and pencil sharpeners and hole-punches and scanners
and fax machines and highlighters and stamps and satellite phones
and binders and glue and pens. But mostly it's about them giving orders in the form of suggestions, and keeping their hands to
themselves, and out where I can see them, at all times.

50. You have a section for comments there on your interview sheet,
right?

51. Good. I want you to write, "He is a man of uncommon attri-
butes and impeccable taste." Write that now, please. Now. Good.
Where it says Personal Appearance, please write *Despampanante.*

52. Yes, it's Spanish.

53. Where it says Accent, write "Heavy regional," but do not indicate the region. Where it says Knowledge of Job-Specific Subject
Matter, write "Vast." Where it says Arm-strength, write "Moderate
to Fairly Strong," and where it says Disposition, if you'd be so kind,
check the boxes indicating "Enthusiastic" and "Friendly."

54. You don't? Bummer.

55. Long-term goals, yes, upper management, definitely. Or else to
own my own business. And also, if she survived somehow, to search
for and eventually, after months and months of searching, right as
I'm about to give up, to find my wife on the South Seas island she
washed up on, and to begin our life together anew there with the
palm trees and coconuts and parrots and papayas and coconuts.

56. Massive human error, tragedy and redemption, definitely. So.
When do I start?

Wait

Waiting Lounge 19A in Wing D of Terminal 4 is precisely full. The airline personnel smile. The loudspeaker voice says that the flight will begin boarding shortly; the announcement is in English, the woman's accent a mix of Portuguese, Dutch, and Malay.

A Canadian accountant snaps his briefcase shut and stares out at the fog that is settling on the tarmac. The fog is dense and gray and certain. He glances at the passengers seated to either side of him—an old Bulgarian man working a crossword puzzle, an older Honduran woman fast asleep—then at the statue in the center of the lounge, a naked boy holding a cell phone and some sort of globular tropical fruit.

The plane is now invisible, but the smiles of the airline personnel do not wane. The accountant wonders if his futures market holdings back home are headed for contango or backwardation. He shivers, walks from his seat to the windows, presses his fingertips to the pane.

The pilot and crew stride into the lounge, consult with the airline personnel, stride back out. The scheduled boarding time comes and goes. The loudspeaker voice announces that the fog will be lifting momentarily.

The accountant returns to his seat, removes a pad of paper from his briefcase, commences doodling. Children take out coloring books. Other passengers unfold newspapers and magazines. Airline personnel daydream of islands, and speak urgently into handheld radios though this is only for show: the batteries have been on backorder for years.

Aircraft scheduled to land circle invisibly overhead. The fog flares against the glass. The Bulgarian clutches his forehead, and the accountant asks if he needs medical assistance.

- No, thank you.
- You're sure?
- Do I look as though I need it?
- A little.

- Yes. I am attempting to think of something for which the flaring of this fog might be metonymically appropriate.

The Canadian squints.

- I am a poet, says the Bulgarian.

- Ah.

- Yes.

The Bulgarian also squints, then shrugs and returns to his crossword. The televisions buzz and mumble, news about a war that is beginning or ending in a country nearby, not the neighboring country to the west but the next one over. All but one of the children close their coloring books and take out their jacks; a small Mongolian boy takes out his checkerboard instead, and worries that this will make him unlikable.

The accountant pulls a scarf from his carry-on, winds it around his neck. Across the lounge sits a girl from Ghana, and she is unthinkably beautiful; he stares at her until he realizes that she is staring back. He looks down, pretends to find a doodle that needs improving, and the girl from Ghana smiles.

The loudspeaker voice announces that there will be a brief delay as the plane's instruments are recalibrated. The Mongolian boy plays himself to a draw; the airline personnel hand out dense cassava crackers and bright purple tea, assure everyone that it will be only a few minutes more, and the air thickens with discontent.

The fog shifts to the left, and back to the right. The televisions brim and burble about soccer. The poet asks the accountant if he knows the name of the Norse goddess who keeps the Apples of Eternal Youth in a box. The accountant apologizes for not knowing. The poet asks if he knows the capital of Bahrain. Again the accountant says that he is sorry. The poet asks if he knows the smell of kyufte as it fries on the stove; the accountant asks how a smell could be a crossword clue, and the poet says it has nothing to do with the puzzle—he hasn't been back to Bulgaria in forty years, and the smell of kyufte is his favorite childhood memory.

The accountant nods and shakes his head. The poet throws the newspaper in a garbage can and goes to sleep. The accountant turns to the old Honduran woman, now awake. She gums a smile at him. He stares out the window again.

The Mongolian boy plays himself to another draw as the other children put away their jacks and take out their comic books. The aircraft circling invisibly overhead are sent to alternate airports. The airline personnel report that the boarding of the flight will be delayed for another hour to allow the fog to lift. The bookstore manager laments not having raised his prices this morning.

Passengers now crowd the gate. Urgencies are explained—pregnant wife, dying father, sick cat, ex-husband in pursuit—and the airline personnel communicate their understanding and deep regret. There is shrieking with spittle in regard to eggplant rotting on a dock in Stockholm, and the poet wakes, scratches his face, shouts *Iduna!* The accountant leans slightly away. The poet roots through the garbage can, pulls out the crossword puzzle, fills in the word.

A bar that has run short of ice negotiates with another that has run short of napkins. The televisions shudder and flash: there has been a chemical spill of some sort just outside the airport. The driver missed his exit because of the fog, says the reporter; a taxi skidded and a bus swerved, the truck jackknifed, and for the moment no one is allowed in or out the main entrance.

Groups form: impatient passengers versus patient passengers. The accountant and the poet are neither patient nor impatient, and pretend to read as the yelling begins.

The loudspeaker voice says that all reports indicate the fog will not lift until early the following morning; that the flight will thus be postponed for precisely fourteen more hours; and that anyone wishing to leave the airport at this time will be escorted out the cargo bay entrance located in Terminal F. The passengers discuss options. The fog flexes. The old Honduran woman gums a smile to no one in particular. The accountant asks the poet if he knows why some of the terminals have numbers and some have letters.

‒ Manama, says the poet.

‒ I beg your pardon?

‒ Manama. Six letters, begins with an M. Yes, it can only be Manama.

The girl from Ghana stretches, and the air around her hums. Night closes in, and the airline personnel report that they are unfortunately unable to offer proper lodging for the evening, as all the hotels in the city are full. None of the passengers believe this. More shouting ensues, and an exodus, all of the locals and a number of hopeful non-locals.

A café runs short of creamer; a restaurant runs short of cheese. The airline personnel announce that each passenger still present will receive free cassava crackers and purple tea for the remainder of his or her stay in the airport. The children are very pleased. The poet asks the airline personnel if all traces of cyanide were removed from the cassava roots before they were ground into flour, is assured that in fact they were.

Pillows and blankets are brought from the invisible plane on the tarmac. Children stretch out on the floor. Parents drape themselves with coats. The girl from Ghana stares at the fog, wondering how many days it will take her ex-husband to track her from Berekum. Bars run short of bitters and the cleaning staff cleans, threading themselves between sleepers and sacks in silence.

The poet elbows the accountant, points to the checkerboard protruding from the Mongolian boy's carry-on. Four hours later, with the score 9-7 in favor of the accountant, the old Honduran woman asks if she might play as well. She wins the next twelve matches, falls asleep mid-move at dawn.

The accountant slides the board back into the child's bag. Other passengers stir and scratch. The members of last night's exodus come traipsing back, the locals smiling, satisfied at having chosen wisely, the non-locals exhausted, mumbling anecdotes of numberless cab rides and the infinite walk back from the cargo bay entrance.

Children whine. Airline personnel bring thin coffee and bad rolls, promise that today is the day, that it is only a question of minutes. The fog appears still denser, still grayer, still more certain. The televisions say that the chemical spill is nearly cleaned up and vehicular traffic will soon be permitted on the access road once again.

And the passengers wait. All the bars have run short of cognac and celery sticks. The accountant follows the girl from Ghana into Duty Free, observes her observing ceremonial daggers, buys a key chain bearing an animal that looks part monkey, part ferret, part partridge—a favored local pet.

The loudspeaker voice whistles briefly. The televisions flip and flap, a cholera epidemic spreading toward the city. Groups are reconfigured: locals versus foreigners. There are hygiene-based accusations, a few punches thrown but none landed.

The children ignore this, chase one another through the wing, and one kicks at a carry-on. Both the child and the carry-on belong to locals, but from different parts of the city, and now the groups split into subgroups, the foreigners based on nationality, the locals based on neighborhood and therefore class. Each subgroup retreats into itself, then expands slightly, seeking more terrain; neither the Canadian nor the Bulgarian fit into any subgroup, and they keep their eyes down, their elbows firmly on their armrests.

More shrieking occurs, and some kickboxing, and a small amount of Tae Kwon Do. It is the Belgians who have the first idea for a way to diminish the tension and pass the time: a congress followed by a pageant. Eyes are rolled, but all subsequent ideas are worse. Delegates are nominated, gather in the bookstore and hammer out agreements, square yardage assigned per capita, dotted borders drawn in masking tape. Magazines are shoplifted, and the bookstore manager flutters.

The pageant: middle-class locals drag the statue to one side, and each subgroup pools its make-up and clothes and advice. The women dress in the restrooms, fight for mirror-space and light. Improvised sashes, Swiss judges, an Italian emcee; the vast gifts of the girl from Ghana deafen the crowd, swing each decision, and even so the Venezuelans protest.

Lunch is worrisome: restaurant prices have trebled and there is no ham to be found. Afterwards, children remove toys from bags. The boys have plastic soldiers, the girls have Barbie dolls, and they all play together at war. The dolls wear stiletto heels, are ten times the size of the soldiers, leave death and destruction in their wakes.

There is a new phenomenon, light seeming to sift through the fog that now appears thinner, striped, not entirely sure. The loudspeaker voice announces that the flight will be departing momentarily. The pilot and crew stride again into the lounge, they nod and wave, and applause floods the air.

Magazines are stowed and carry-ons are hefted, hands are shaken and a line forms. The line lengthens, and yet there is no cutting in. The line arcs and straightens. The boarding-gate door is opened, then closed.

An upper-middle-class local child points out the window. The fog has thickened, darkened, grown more assured.

The pilot and crew stride again out of the lounge, and they do not nod, and they do not wave. The loudspeaker voice announces that the flight will be delayed momentarily. The subgroups sulk back to their territories. Children poke each other and cry.

An hour passes this way, and another hour, and another. The bookstore manager aligns his paperbacks. The fog surges, stalls, surges. The Mongolian boy comes to the accountant, asks what is in his briefcase, says that he hopes to be an accountant when he grows up, or else a matador, and then his mother calls and he runs away.

The old woman from Honduras champs and sighs and dreams of a pageant she once won, a pageant that never occurred, but it was wonderful, wonderful; she waved to the throng, thanked her father for his unwavering support, and the poet turns to the accountant.

- Would you happen to know—
- No.
- I was only wondering—
- It doesn't matter. The answer is no.

The Bulgarian shrugs, Afghanistan's longest river goes unnamed, and there is an explosion not far away; children fall and parents stumble, the lounge windows crack, ceiling tiles pinwheel through the air and dust pours into the wing, the lights go out and the televisions fall dark, there is shouting and screaming and hands clawing at necks and eyes.

Then there is the hum and grind of generators, and the electricity returns, and the passengers go still.

The loudspeaker voice requests that all available security guards and cleaning staff report immediately to their respective central work stations. Airline personnel run in medium-sized circles. The passengers gather around the televisions that clatter and spark. They wait and wait and at last the answer comes: a small meteor has hit the main lobby.

It is not easy to believe, but the images are undeniable. Delegates meet at the boarding gate and reach no conclusions. Children kick one another. Restaurants run short of lettuce. The loudspeaker voice announces that for security reasons no one will be permitted to leave the premises until further notice.

The airline personnel assure the passengers that there is no reason to panic, that while the number of dead and wounded is not yet known, there is no structural damage to Wing D, and the plane and runway and control tower are wholly intact, and it is therefore only a question of the fog lifting and then the flight will be on its way.

Passengers wander out to see the meteor and damage, are met by armed guards and partitioning, wander back. The Honduran woman finds a large fuchsia bug crawling up her pant leg; it has nine eyes and twenty-two legs, reminds her of her mother's flower garden, and she squashes it with her fist. Bars run short of swizzle sticks, and then, improbably, gin.

The fog scurls. Toilets clog and garbage cans overflow. Darkness drops, the generators growl and fail, and the airline personnel regret that no additional blankets are available. The subgroups gather into themselves. The girl from Ghana dreams the roar of a thousand fontomfrom drums while across the lounge the accountant fights through a nightmare involving misconstrued negative amortization schedules.

In the morning there is still no electricity, and the subgroups curse and pace. There are accusations of theft—missing magazines, missing mints. The fog slackens, then stiffens, and at the masking-tape borders there are dark suggestions, darker looks.

The local delegates gather in a sloppy oval, announce that they have had enough, that they are going home, that they will break down the door if necessary, will walk across the tarmac and scale any fence and be free. The airline personnel insist that the flight will be departing at any moment. The locals gather their things. The airline personnel take a stand at the boarding gate. The locals push them aside, then hesitate: lined outside the door are a dozen soldiers standing shadowed and gray in the fog.

The locals look at the airline personnel. The airline personnel shrug and say that they have no idea either. The locals set down their things, gather again. The soldiers grimace and strut. The airline personnel wave the unit captain up to the glass, and words are passed, and the words are diffuse, something about a quarantine, but its cause is unclear: the word 'virus' is heard, but what came before? AIDS? Space?

The locals froth. An hour passes angrily. The fog lifts eight inches, drops back down. The Bulgarian rereads an old poem in his notebook, contemplates adding an adverb, and the Belgians have another idea: an Olympiad.

Enough already, say the Dutch. And yet no better idea is brought forward. Judges are appointed, and passengers who belong to no subgroup are assigned to one now created: Other. A program is drawn up on stationery bought by the Saudis; the Americans want baseball, the Russians want volleyball, the Chinese want table tennis, and all are disappointed. The upper-lower-middle-class locals suggest that children ride their parents for the equestrian events.

Synchronized swimming is exchanged for synchronized walking; water polo becomes carpet polo, and archery is replaced with Throw the Ball of Paper into the Garbage Can from Increasingly Great Distances. Winter events are ignored until the Norwegians threaten to boycott; then babies in strollers are called bobsledders, and curling is given pride of place and time.

Hog lines are drawn in chalk, brooms are taken from closets, wheeled carry-on bags replace rocks, and the Scottish skip's hammer is a double takeout draw for the gold. Next comes fencing, a question of umbrellas; then rowing occurs with baggage carts and mops, and the Australian coxless four is untouchable.

Dressage is won by a Chilean toddler when the Mongolian boy's father hashes a last-minute piaffe. Kenyans of course sweep the marathon, hours of quick circling; Cubans of course sweep the boxing. A Turk and a Greek meet in judo, half-middleweight the only division: the Greek has mastered the body drop, the naked strangle, and the inner thigh, but the Turk has mastered the sweeping hip, the scarf hold, and both the major inner and major outer reaps, thereby carrying the day and declaring the Cyprus question settled.

The Latvians are accused of doping, the Nigerians of bribery. A tenor from Surinam sings so that rhythmic gymnastics might flourish. Again there is a small amount of Tae Kwon Do, the lower-upper-upper-class locals upsetting the Koreans to everyone's moderate surprise.

The members of Other are the Canadian, the Bulgarian, five stout young women who are not willing to say where they are from, an Orthodox priest from Ukraine, and a lawyer from Pakistan. They consistently come in fourth. The Canadian apologizes for his failure to hurdle more deftly, and his teammates tell him not to worry as long as he did his best, which they are sure he did. The girl from Ghana blows him a kiss from the long jump pit, and the fog brindles and shies.

The competition lasts until nightfall the following day. The medal ceremony is light-hearted yet dignified, and the medals donated by Duty Free are foil-wrapped chocolate coins that gleam in the low gray light. The members of Other admire their Participant ribbons. The airline personnel announce that 19A is surely the greatest intact lounge in the entire airport. Free purple tea for everyone!

But in the morning: post-Olympic malaise. The five women announce that they will no longer be known as Other, that such marginalization will not be tolerated in this day, and this age. No one is listening. The restaurants and bars and cafes have run short of most things; what were meant to be in-flight meals are defrosted in the plane on the tarmac, brought and handed out. Spouses bitch to and at one another. Parents smack children, generally their own but not always. The Honduran woman snorts. Still there is no electricity; still the fog hangs.

The accountant gets up, walks past the girl from Ghana, stands looking out the window. The girl from Ghana smiles. The accountant sees the smile reflected in the cracked glass, turns, attempts conversation.

They discuss the man from New Guinea and the woman from Guinea-Bissau, unknown to each other until this wait, and the Ukrainian priest who now weds them; they discuss the man from Madrid and the woman from Warsaw, eight years of marriage, of bickering and contempt, and the Pakistani lawyer who draws up the papers for their divorce. They discuss the soldiers and the statue, the meteor and the fog. They do not, however, discuss their respective ex-spouses: warlord currently closing in, librarian currently dating a podiatrist.

A young Bolivian woman gives birth in the bookstore, the manager himself delivering, while in a restroom an old Kazakh man is bitten by a tiny blue snake—a species of viper says one local, a species of adder says another. The viper or adder escapes through a crack in the tile; the Kazakh dies and is buried in a planter. Then night swells. The priest agrees to swap seats with the accountant in exchange for a fountain pen. The accountant puts his arm around the girl, feels the thick chaotic scars on her far shoulder, wonders; they slump together, sleep, snore.

The next morning, again there are things to discuss: Cubans, for example. The Cubans are up to something. They have been gathered since well before dawn, whispering, and now are approaching each of the other subgroups, and whispering again. Finally one comes to where the accountant and the girl from Ghana sit.

- It is time, whispers their Cuban, a thin boy perhaps nine years old.
- Time for what? says the accountant.
- Time to go.
- Go where?

- To the plane.
- What for?
- My uncle is a trained pilot. My cousin is a trained stewardess. We will fly the plane ourselves.
- But how do we know if the plane even has fuel? And what if mechanical difficulties occur? Have you considered the possibility of in-flight mechanical difficulties?
- All possibilities have been considered. My aunt is a trained aircraft technician. My brother is a trained philosopher but has worked at a gas station.
- What about the quarantine?
- It does not interest us.
- And the soldiers?
- We do not think they will try to stop us once they see our determination.
- But if they do?
- That will be unfortunate. Very, very unfortunate. It is the price that must be paid, however. You do not have to join us. We are not asking you to join us. You are welcome to join us if you wish, but you are also free not to join us, if that is your desire.

The girl from Ghana stands; the accountant catches her arm, shakes his head. She sits back down, watches as the Cubans are joined by a number of other passengers, all of them childless, all of them medalists: an ululating rhombus of discontent. The locals, too, have formed a rhombus, a separate and smaller rhombus; it appears that they intend to take advantage of the Cuban commotion, to escape across the tarmac and climb any fence as planned.

The soldiers' expressions are not clearly visible in the fog. The larger rhombus slides toward the boarding-gate door. The airline personnel attempt dissuasion, promising limitless purple tea, and also mauve tea, and even the rare chartreuse tea, if the Cubans and childless medalists will just have a little patience.

The larger rhombus shouts and charges, the smaller rhombus slips in behind, the boarding-gate door is broken down; shouts and flashes fill the fog, and it can only be imagined, some soldiers beaten to the ground, others crouched and firing, the running and falling, the gurgle of death, the scrambling and standing and running once again.

Another sound now: the sound of jet engines! The accountant and the girl from Ghana hug one another and cry, ashamed of their cowardice, though thrilled for those who have triumphed. The scream of the engines dissipates, and surely the plane is trundling out to the runway; the scream returns, louder and louder and the plane must now be going airborne and then an explosion as loud as that of the meteor, and the brightest of muffled flashes, and in the light of that flash is a moment when all can just be seen: the plane has hit the control tower.

The accountant and the girl from Ghana hug one another again, and cry again, no longer thrilled or ashamed. They hold each other through the numb silence, and the shrieks, and the wailing, and the Mongolian boy stares from where he hides beneath his seat.

All eyes close for a time. When they open again, airline personnel are repairing the door, and soldiers are once more visible out the windows, though fewer of them and in some disarray. The remaining subgroups return to their territories, extend their boundaries, claim two seats per passenger.

There is no food or drink to be had in any bar, café or restaurant; the remaining delegates gather, discuss, and ransack Duty Free. The spoils are distributed equitably, chocolate and champagne and cigarettes for all. Again the fog flares. The poet takes out his notebook, scribbles at length, hides the scribbling with his hand when the Honduran woman leans close, and now the airline personnel announce that they have good news: the Cubans and childless medalists took the wrong plane, and the remaining passengers' flight will be departing momentarily, just as soon as the fog lifts and the electricity is restored and the quarantine is ended and the control tower is rebuilt.

All of the women in the lounge begin menstruating simultaneously; a tampon is worth a bottle of champagne, then two bottles, then a case. The men of each subgroup huddle, discuss suicide. The cold has gone treacherous, and as darkness at last descends, all extra seats are destroyed for fuel. The bookstore is dismembered for kindling, the manager at first resisting, then remembering his insurance and standing aside. Each fire is tended gently, but in the morning there are new claims of theft—missing Marlboros, missing Kents.

The delegates meet desperately; the Belgian suggests a spelling bee and is beaten senseless. The girl from Ghana tells the Canadian that things will soon go bad, that she has been in similar situations, and always things go bad. She asks if he has any skills that might be useful.

- I'm a whiz at analyzing debenture impact on leverage.
- Anything else?
- I've been known to make adequate preparations for balloon maturity.

Just then, on the far side of the wing, the Greek defeats the Turk at tic-tac-toe, announces that the Cyprus question has been reopened. The Turk pushes the Greek. The Greek pushes the Turk. Sides are drawn up, only two of them now, and there is punching and kickboxing and Tae Kwon Do, there is pinching and biting and scratching, the soldiers kick down the boarding-gate door, are attacked by passengers bearing burning armrests and broken bottles of Moët et Chandon, the girl from Ghana drags the accountant into a corner and lays herself across him, there is automatic weapons fire and the jolt of grenades, shouting and screams and then silence.

The girl from Ghana lifts her head. She asks the accountant if he is all right, and he says that he thinks he is. Together they stand. There is a gash in the girl's right forearm, and the accountant binds it with his scarf. Nothing else moves but dust. They walk through the lounge, and the statue of the boy with his cell phone and globular fruit is perfectly intact against the far wall, but all else is shattered glass, strangled soldiers, torn carpet, impaled passengers, broken brooms, disemboweled airline personnel.

The accountant stumbles over the Honduran woman, her neck bent obliquely. He closes her eyes and mouth, hears a slight moan to his left, and finds the poet bleeding from the chest, his bare feet burned black, tendrils of smoke extending from each toe.

- That is it, says the poet.
- What is what?
- The smell of kyufte as it fries on the stove.
- But there is no kyufte here.
- There is. There must be. It can only be kyufte.

The accountant takes the poet in his arms, shakes his head but then he knows: it is the smell of the poet's own charred flesh. He tells the Bulgarian that he is right, that it is kyufte, the finest kyufte ever fried, and the waiter will be arriving at any moment to serve them. The Bulgarian nods and dies. The accountant lays him down.

There is light and sputtering from many directions: the electricity has returned. The televisions declare that the national cricket team has finally gotten its new uniforms. The girl from Ghana finds another survivor, the Mongolian boy, and she brushes the glass from his hair and picks him up.

The loudspeaker voice clears its throat, announces that the departure of their flight will be delayed momentarily. There is a thump, and another, and the Mongolian boy points. The accountant and the girl from Ghana look. Something large and brown is smacking against the window frame.

They step to the boarding-gate door. Before them is a massive rattan basket hanging half a foot off the ground. Loose tethers writhe to either side. The balloon itself can barely be seen, a vast round dense yellow presence above them, and the basket slumps and settles as they watch.

- You told me that you are an expert with balloons, says the girl from Ghana.
- I— Not balloon-balloons. Balloon maturity. It's—
- Balloons are balloons. It is not a difficult thing.
- Right, but—
- Owuraku.
- Well, be that as it may—
- My ex-husband.

The accountant follows her eyes. Working toward them is a very tall, very black, heavily armed man whose expression oscillates between rage and despair. He searches from body to statue to bookstore. He glances at the boarding-gate door.

Now the girl from Ghana climbs into the basket, sets the Mongolian boy down, flips switches at random. The pilot light ignites. The girl from Ghana reads labeling, fires the burner, looks at the accountant. From deep in the fog comes a voice shouting about the difference between hands on and light hands on. The warlord is now pacing toward the door.

The accountant climbs in, and the Mongolian boy comes to stand beside him. The girl from Ghana tosses ballast. The basket begins to lift. The accountant tells the boy that there is nothing to be afraid of, taps at the gauges for the pyrometer, the altimeter and the variometer, wonders what they signify and hopes they are not important.

The warlord appears at the door. The accountant reels in the tethers. The warlord screams and falls and begs. The air smells of kyufte. The basket rises into the cold wet gray, and the warlord weeps, aims, fires, misses, beautifully.

Triangulation

*E*ighteen years on the force, I seen plenty of, you know, but nothing like that. The dead ones was frozen solid so there wasn't much stink, but imagine if it'd been a few weeks later, things starting to thaw out.... And the noise, it was—the ones that was still alive, they could barely stand up but they was still bellowing. It just never stopped.

ᴇᴐ

A month or so, I imagine. Maybe longer. The barn's right out there in back, of course. The first time? I honestly don't remember. But it would have been like any other day. Up at five, freezing cold outside, get dressed and then something must have... And from then on I couldn't. But don't you dare think I didn't try.

ᴇᴐ

The whole barn was full of frozen manure, ankle-deep, even deeper. And it wasn't just manure neither. Maybe ten of the cows had died while they was birthing, the calves half-way out, dead as dead gets.

ᴇᴐ

I still dream about them sometimes. Once or twice a week, sometimes more. I— No, nothing like that. Just the sound. I'll be dreaming, and— Well, that's the thing, I can never remember. Just regular dreams I guess, but then I hear them, and I know it's a dream but I can't, I try but I can't wake up, and the noise gets louder and louder.

ᴇᴐ

Virginia. Little town you never heard of outside Roanoke. Not too bad a place, but I don't think I'll ever…. Nothing waiting for me down there. Anyway, this guy's barn, there wasn't a scrap of hay anywhere. No oats, no hay, nothing. Must've been ninety head at the beginning but there was only maybe thirty or so still alive when I got there, and some of them was almost gone. The officer who came out to handle things while I took the guy to the station, he told me later he had to put a bunch of them down.

℘

I should have auctioned them off years ago. And those things I told you a minute ago, I hope you didn't get the idea…. That whole thing about getting up at five— Yes, but that was part of what I loved about it. Yes, freezing, but you do it anyway, you pull on your boots, you head out and the cows are there like always, rumbling now and then, swinging a hip against you as you hook them up. We— Look, you can believe whatever you want, but— I know, but, look, just listen to me for a second. There was this guy, old Schoen, who used to work for us. Once when I was about, I don't know, eleven or so, I saw him take an electric prod to one of our cattle and I just, I couldn't, I saw how the cow jumped and I just went after him. I climbed up his back and he threw me off but I got up and went after him again, swinging my fists, tears all down my face, and he just let me swing. Old Schoen. I wonder what ever happened to him.

℘

Well, so just for argument's sake let's say that's how it was. Okay. But there's always a way out. Did I ever tell you what happened with those two hitchhikers?

℘

Dad let me look at the ledger but he never explained it to me. When I won the scholarship he made me promise I'd come back as soon as I graduated, work the farm until the— English lit. Do you ever read poetry? There's this great poem by Wordsworth. "Whether we be young or old / Our destiny, our being's heart and home, / is with infinity, and only there; / With…" No, that's not, that's not quite it. There's a— Syracuse. Best four years of my life. Yes, but Dad and I had a deal. And I thought I knew what I was in for, but the business side— Well, I don't know. He probably just thought there would be time. He was only sixty-four, tough as they come. So that was probably it. Unless.... No, I was just thinking, there was this family over in Ithaca, and the boy, I don't remember exactly but he came back from college, took charge of the farm, finally had his dad sign the herd and the property over. Then a few months later he up and sold.

☙

Yeah, well, the report don't tell half of it. They just waited by the side of the road and as soon as somebody stopped, bang, bullet to the back of the head. Money, jewelry, stereo, whatever they could carry. Anyway, I finally caught up with them. Blew by them out on 126 west of Carthage and I knew it was them. I— Well, no, but there was two of them and they looked a little rotten and I just knew somehow. So I radioed in and whipped back around, but by then a car had already stopped. I threw on the lights and the siren but now the guys had these folks hostage, baby in the back seat, I don't know what-all. And it was just me out there, you understand? One of the guys stayed with the couple, gun to the woman's neck, husband on the ground now with his head bashed in, and the other guy took off into the trees and started circling back toward me. He— Well, yeah, but there's that one big stand maybe a quarter-mile long, maple and poplar and, I don't know, white pine or something. I couldn't see to get a shot off and the other one's holding the woman, screaming how he'll waste her if I don't drop the piece. You want to talk about trapped? I— Look, just let me finish the story, okay? You know what I did? Do you? I put a bullet through the motherfucker's forehead. No, not the, the guy with the woman. Thirty yards, off-hand. So then the other guy starts shooting, puts one through the window and this big fucking chip of glass jags into my cheek. They're not supposed to break like that—they're made out of some special, I don't know, anyway I'm bleeding all over the place and this guy keeps coming. So I put him down too. One in the stomach, four in the face. Don't talk to me about trapped.

☙

Definitely not. Not back then. Hard work, sure, but that's what I was born to. There's this other poem, Walt Whitman, you've probably heard it. "…Toil, healthy toil and sweat, endless, without cessation, / The old, old practical burdens, interests, joys…" The way it goes from there, of course, I never, but that's exactly what it felt like, or so I believed. So I convinced myself to believe. No, strike that, I take that back. I really did believe it. All those folks who live in cities, they have no idea, they, no idea where milk comes from. So, no, not back then. Yes. Five years ago, give or take. Five years last December.

⁊

I don't know exactly. Anonymous tip, I imagine. A neighbor or somebody must've stopped by, seen the cattle, how they was, ribs sticking out like I don't know what. And the neighbor or whoever gets pissed off, makes a anonymous call, and I went out to check on it. Wasn't the first time neither from what I heard. The sheriff's office sent somebody out there a couple of times, but nobody wrote him up. Felt sorry for him I guess.

⁊

Yes, exactly. And it was hard. Hard on me, hard on Mom. She— Sixty-one. No, sixty-two. Sorry, yes, sixty-two.

⁊

You know what was the weirdest thing of all? Well, maybe not the weirdest, but pretty fucking strange. The guy still lives with his mother. He— Oh, she died a few years after my daddy. I was about eighteen. Nineteen, maybe—I was already out of school. Well, it was kind of a mess, drugs and whatnot, but then I did a stint in the Marines. No, I just missed it. My brother went, though, machine-gunner on a Huey, came back even more fucked up than when he left. Anyway, four years in the Marines and then back in Roanoke, didn't really know what to do, headed north for the hell of it, did some odd jobs, you know, whatever came along. The truth of it, though, a guy gets used to being in uniform. They've got this academy down in Troy, nothing too tough compared to boot camp. And I've been plugging away ever since. Nope, just me and the wife. We tried for a while, but there was, I don't know, something didn't quite.... Sure, we thought about it, but you hear so many stories, family adopts a kid and it turns out his folks was psychos or whatever and the kid's got the bad genes—he starts out killing cats, tossing them on his neighbor's porch like newspapers and a few years later you're hearing about him on TV.

 ❧

No. I'd always hoped to, of course, but there isn't much in the way of— Sorry, is your wife from around here? Boston? Fine town, Boston. Oh, just once or twice while I was in college. Anyway, I'd hoped to find someone once I got back here, but the local girls, I don't know, they, well, I never found anyone quite right. And with dairy farming you end up so tired you don't even want to, you know, you just don't have the energy left over to pick up the phone and dial the number. And after Dad died, of course, out of the question, too much work, too much worry. Who'd want to buy into a thing like that?

❧

Right, and his mother. I never went up to see her but the guy from Social Services said she was in pretty bad shape—he had to tell her about a hundred times who he was and why they had to go.

❧

Bankruptcy? No. Because I'm my father's son, that's why. I know, but I'd made a promise and I— Well, no, but I had to keep trying. Right, but I couldn't even, look, I haven't had a solid night's sleep in five years.

❧

So he had it tough. If he'd watched himself a little better— Well, hell, he could've sold the herd, or maybe leased the property to somebody who knew what the hell they was doing. I found out later there's even a telephone hotline for farmers in trouble. All you have to do is call, and that fucker never did. What, in the same situation? Well, I'd, absolutely, you're goddamn right I would. You think there's a hotline for state troopers? Oh, counseling, sure, but the guy who runs it, skinny little prick sits back in his chair and asks if your daddy used to— No. Well, yeah, once. A couple of months ago, right after the thing with the hitchhikers. It's mandatory after any kind of fatal shooting. Right. They said that once he was on the ground I should've— Well, sure, but you weren't there, were you? You didn't have a piece of goddamn glass stuck in your face, and you didn't see the— No, but he still had his— Will you let me finish my sentence? Will you? Thank you. He still had the gun in his hand and his eyes was open and he, it looked like he was raising the gun. I know. But you weren't there.

℘

Yes, I'm aware of that. I don't know why I, I've asked myself that very question, and I don't know, I just felt like.... No, more like I'd already accepted too much help, more than Dad ever would have. Yes, I realize that now. But Dad— No, yes, you're right. Of course you're right.

℘

So I told them I wasn't going back, and they said okay but I had to find somebody else and pay for it myself, and you know what's even worse? Here I am paying you fifty goddamn dollars an hour, and a guy who starves his cattle to death gets his head shrunk for free. How's that for ironic. I, yeah, it was part of his sentence. How the hell should I know? Some shrink from Carthage maybe, or one of those Cornell— Okay, no, but the state paid for everything else, didn't it? Guy gets off scot-free, practically, and I'll bet you he's living off unemployment right this— Oh, a couple of months I guess. Couldn't pay his bail, and once it went to court he wouldn't hardly let his lawyer speak. Right, but since he was a first-time offender and all that. Exactly. End of story.

℘

Now? I don't have the faintest idea. We're going to lose everything but the house, and we've still got all the back taxes. But you know what I'd really like to do? Teach poetry. I can't imagine anything— No, I guess they wouldn't, but maybe somewhere else, some other state, find a little private high school somewhere. Or go back to college, get my master's, even a doctorate. I suppose not. Oh, some days are better than others. Back when the cattle were still, when they were, she heard the noise and sometimes she thought... Look, I know how this is going to sound, but, well, she thought they were singing. To her. She'd call me up to her room and ask if I'd been, if.... But it wasn't always like that. Sometimes she knew something was wrong, and she'd ask. I don't remember what I told her. Mastitis, maybe. It's an infection—if you don't milk them often enough their udders block up, get inflamed. If you just let it go? High fever, the cow stops eating. Anyway. Mom can't get out of bed anymore, so— No, I suppose not.

ɛⁿɔ

Yeah, I know, but could you give me till the beginning of next month? Great. Thank you. I should be able to get ahead by then, but right now— Well, my wife's talking about starting a little mail-order business. I don't know, jams, jellies, that sort of thing. She does this elderberry jam what would make your— I don't know. She's just looking into it now. Who knows if it'll all work out or not, but at least she's trying. She's a hard worker. We both are. And that's all it takes, right?

ɛⁿɔ

Is it? Well, fine then. Right, you too. Well, I don't know exactly how much, but, yes, I really think it is. I— But next week we'll be— Really, if you wouldn't mind I'd just as soon— Have you been listening to me? Have you, how many times do I have to— Okay. No, fine, one more time: I tried. Every single day. But then there was a day when— No, not the exact, does that seem like the kind of thing you'd mark on your calendar? Okay then. And from that day on— Because there wasn't any point. There was nothing I could give them. A man can only.... Nothing. No, nothing. I just remembered the first day. Or, no, not the first day I couldn't, but the last day I could. It was one of those mornings when the air is so cold it hurts to breathe. Weeks since I'd had anything to give them. And right up until that day, every morning when I went out, the cattle, they always look up when they hear you coming, they know you're there to feed them and.... But it had been weeks, and on that last day they didn't even look up.

❧

You know what got to me the worst? Well, but besides that. It was how he looked at me when I asked him. Right, I asked him straight up and he just stared at me. Didn't make any excuses, just stared at me like he— I don't know. And you know what he did then? The fucker smiled at me. Which, at the time you can imagine how bad I wanted to pop him. But now when I think about it— Yup. All the time. Anyway, that smile of his, but I'm almost sure it wasn't what I thought. Well, you know, like he was making fun of me or— When I first got there? I knocked on the door but nobody answered so I went and had a look around the barn, saw all those cattle, the live ones still bleating, the dead ones frozen solid, all the calves, and by then I was pissed, I was ready to— I don't think so. No, I kept it, I definitely kept it in the holster. Anyway, when I came out of the barn I saw him standing there on his back porch, and I walked right up and asked him what the hell was going on, and he didn't say anything at all. I can't tell you how bad I wanted him to, I don't know, make a run for it, or even just give some kind of excuse. But there was nothing like that. He just looked at me, and that smile, which I'm thinking now.... That he was glad it was over. He'd, whatever happened to him, I don't know, he was just glad it was over. But like I say, right then if he'd so much as— No, I know, but sometimes you get so pissed off, you see something like that and you— I realize that. Of course. Yeah, I, well, why the hell do you think I'm here right now talking to you? I— What, already?

[*Exeunt.*

*T*he birds are catching fire again. I keep shouting up to them, Fly lower, fly lower! They never listen. They're dropping all around us now, and we run for the nearest building, this big squat red thing, a county office of some kind, maybe something to do with zoning? But the door is locked and no one comes no matter how loud we knock so we cover our heads and run across the street to this cheesy trattoria-type thing and huddle there under the awning, or what should be an awning, red-and-white striped, but isn't—there's nothing left but shreds after the big birdstorm last week. So we open our tin umbrellas, hold them over our heads, close our eyes. The birds smack into the pavement, and I try to guess the species from how much noise they make when they hit. I feel Xanthe coming closer. She takes my free hand in hers; I don't open my eyes, and wonder if hers are still closed. I wait. Then something huge whacks into the side of the fake-a-toria only a few feet away and we both flinch. Noise like that, it had to have been at least a goose. Would have crushed these umbrellas and our heads like a mace or maybe a flail. I think about that for a moment, and it's nice—death, the two of us together, as long as her eyes are closed when the goose strikes. The air is acrid with the smell of burnt feathers and it's getting hard to breathe. Are you okay? I ask. Fine and dandy, she says. We wait. There are a few more medium-sized crunches but nothing close enough to feel dangerous. Then there's a moment or two of silence, and I keep waiting—a long moment more, another. Finally I open my eyes. Hers are already open but that means nothing necessarily. Okay then, she says. She lets go of my hand, closes her umbrella, stands staring at me until I realize she's waiting for me to close mine too. So I do. And she takes my hand again and we walk up the street and are careful not to look down at the blackish piles. She's very good at sidestepping without looking down. She points at a shop window where there's this nice green dress, and I think she's hoping that some day I'll get it for her as a surprise. Then there's a faint whistling sound. It grows louder and louder and ends with a small thump at my feet: a hummingbird of some kind, now nothing but a knot of ash and sinew. I check the sky, and the storm's well and truly over—this was just the last drop. I squat down and Xanthe asks what the hell I'm doing. I reach out and she says Don't you dare touch it. I pick it up, turn it over, brush away as much of what's burned as I can. Traces of an emerald gorget, a hint of white collar, indigo belly. I tell Xanthe that it's hard to be sure but I think it's a Hyacinth Visorbearer. She looks at me. God-damnit, she says, I told you to leave it alone. If you keep doing shit like this, I'm going to have to, I'll, I'm, and then she stops talking and I look at her and she walks away.

LEAD ACTOR: I think my leg's broken. Does it look bro-ken to you? It is, isn't it? Unbelievable.

Dies.

Liesl saw an internet ad for a universal television turner-offer. It was advertised as a universal turner-onner, but she knew what it was really for. It had never occurred to her to want one before but she wanted one now and put in her credit card details and address and a week later it came. Long and thin and gray, no buttons for chan-nels or volume or programming, just the one button, On/Off. She put in the batteries, pointed it at her television, and was a little sur-prised that the thing actually worked: on and off, on and off. She smiled and went to look for her purse and for the first few days she used the device only to build small spaces for herself. Laundromat, waiting room, bus terminal, and if no one else was watching she'd turn off the closest set, construct silence. Slowly she got bolder. The flat-screen at the entrance to the elevator in her apartment build-ing, even if others were watching—it never showed anything but ads anyway. The watchers' faces flickered as the screen went dark, but elevator etiquette was already in place and no one looked at anyone else. Then when she went out to buy a lamp to replace the one by her bedside, which worked perfectly except that it buzzed ever so faint-ly even after she turned it off, in the store's home electronics section she saw a whole wall of televisions, and she extinguished them all with a single click. The elderly couple who had been comparing, de-ciding, they looked at each other, at the clerk. He apologized, turned the televisions back on one by one. She turned them all off again. The clerk started to sweat, said that he'd be right back with the manuals, and the couple shook their heads, wandered away. This was nice, but still inconclusive; the first clear evidence that the world was improving did not arrive until the afternoon she came upon a small crowd standing on the sidewalk, watching a replay of the previous night's Oscar ceremony through the window of a Chinese restaurant. The door was open and the volume was turned up high, but with the traffic and chatter and birds it was still hard to hear what was being said by the man in the tuxedo at the podium on the screen behind the window. She had heard rumors of strange occurrences during the ceremony that had been censored out of the broadcast—a flasher, a fistfight on stage, a speech full of profanity that thanked only the actor's enemies—and other rumors that non-censored versions were out and about. The crowd grew bigger. Then a man in a raincoat ran up the aisle toward the podium, and the woman turned off the television. There were groans from the crowd. She feigned a similar dismay, and waited, and everyone else waited too, hoping, and then drifted away, but there were two young men on opposite sides of the crowd, unknown to each other as far as the woman could tell, and after everyone else had gone and it was just the three of them, one of the men asked the other if he wanted to maybe go get a cup of coffee. So, love. And the world was quieter than it would have been at a few tiny points for a few minutes each day. But of course they caught her in the end. As many need the noise as don't, she learned. A sports bar this time, bottom of the eighth and runners at the corners, a two-two count, the wind-up, the pitch, the flare of darkness. The watchers shouted and spun. The bartender turned the set back on, and she turned it off again, and the watchers snarled and hissed. On again and off, on and off, the snarling went jagged and then someone realized that she was the only one who hadn't been rooting for either team. Someone else had seen the internet ad too, made the connection, ripped her purse out of her hands and emptied it on the table, snatched the universal control and held it up, then grabbed an imitation antique golf club from its wall mount and beat the woman to death. There was blood on the wall, on the napkins, on the cardboard coasters, and there were bits of teeth on the floor. The murder made the news that night, and the two young men who'd met on the sidewalk in front of the Chinese restaurant looked at each other, wondered, tried to decide if they remembered the woman's face. They couldn't be sure. They only remembered each other. They shook their heads and laughed, and then went quiet. They shook their heads again. They kissed, but then no. So they spooned together and did not sleep well.

DIRECTOR: Fuck. Fuck fuck fuck fuck fuck. Now what
                     do we do? Seriously. Anybody? Any ideas?
                     Now what the fuck do we do?

We finally left her about a year ago. We shouldn't have, but we just
couldn't deal with it anymore. Nobody could have, is what we tell
ourselves. Later we went back and she was gone. Or not gone, exactly, but way beyond our reach.

UNDERSTUDY: I know all his lines.

DIRECTOR: You cunt. You stupid fucking cunt. I know
                     you know his lines. I know you fucking
                     know his fucking lines, all right? I'm not
                     talking about his lines. I'm talking about
                     this, this, this *body*, and all this fucking
                     blood.

The kid backed away but kept his eyes on the man, and the man
held up his hands and said What the hell! It wasn't like he'd done
anything wrong—he'd just been walking, whatever, not really paying much attention, turned the corner and bam! Smacked right into
the kid, who from the look of things hadn't been paying much attention either. Now there was water all over the man's shirt. The
kid was maybe nine and his eyes were scared wide open, as if he
thought the man was going to rob or molest him. The man said
Hey, kid, watch where you're going. That scared the kid even more,
and he started backing away a little faster. Then the man saw what
the kid was carrying. Just a regular little round fish bowl, half full of
water, the rest of which the man had on his shirt except for a sprin-
kling on the kid's own tank top. Inside the bowl was a goldfish, but
the man had never seen one like this before—it wasn't orange like a
regular goldfish, but gold-colored, the actual color of gold. The man
stared at it, and it got smaller and smaller as the kid backed away,
and the whole thing must have turned into a game for the kid at
some point because otherwise he'd have turned and walked or run
but instead he stayed facing the man, backing away, backing and
backing, and now the man couldn't see the bowl anymore but there
was something weird with the light and he could still see the fish,
not fish-shaped by then, just this spot of gold suspended between
the kid's hands, and the kid still backing away, and the gold was now

a tiny point but still bright and floating there in front of the kid like magic or magnets or something and the man thought If that spot of gold disappears I will go home and put a bullet in my ear because it will finally be time. Then the kid must have tripped over something, stupid stupid kid, backing away like that not looking where he was going, and the spot of gold disappeared and the kid was a long way away but the man could still hear the bowl break.

SUPPORTING ACTOR: Look, it was an accident. Not like it was murder or anything. Accidents happen. We call the police and we tell them the truth. Why are you so—

DIRECTOR: An accident that will cost the studio millions. Will cost me millions. And you, you think you're getting off so easy? You were the one holding the fucking ladder. That's negligence. That's jail-time. I go down, we all go down, motherfucker.

SUPPORTING ACTOR: Hold on. Just hold on now. My *character* was holding the ladder. I was *acting*, in case you didn't notice. *Acting* at holding the ladder. How was I supposed to know I was supposed to be actually holding it? No way. I'm out of here.

DIRECTOR: Don't you dare fucking leave. You stupid fucking fuck, don't you dare fucking—

SUPPORTING ACTOR leaves the set. Door closes behind him, its hydraulic wheeze barely audible.

DIRECTOR: Fuck. Fuck fuck fuck fuck fuck.

You forget that everything is less clear than it seems and then they find this thing and you are reminded. Or found it years ago, decades, but then that whole mess, farmers and dealers and foundations and thieves, prosecutors named Paolo, a hotel room in Geneva and post-dated checks, sixteen years in a safe-deposit box in

Hicksville. Hicksville, the name of the actual town! Then National Geogoddamngraphic and a thousand scattered fragments of papyrus humidified, tweezed into floating alignment between plates of glass. Radiocarbon work, multispectral imaging, paleography and codicology, the ink a mixture of iron gall and soot and finally yes, okay, authentic if hardly true. Because not that it was new in the other sense either: there was the original that got Irenaeus so hot and bothered, plus those possible readings of Mark and John, et cetera. Even Borges got in on the game, wasn't it Borges? Or Cortázar? But so now unquestionably authentic and you should have learned Coptic you stupid old drunk so you wouldn't have to trust all these pussified commentators. But, so…Borges, definitely Borges. But so, and of course it's all nonsense, nothing that can be taken seriously in any theological sense, but it reminds you of the other mess, the real mess: you pick the best man for the hardest job, and Jesus picked Judas. If the cross is part of the plan then betrayal is part of the plan then betrayer is part of the plan. Thirty silver pieces my ass. But loyalty, sure. Friendship, faith. And pride too, maybe, hence the "you will exceed" and "you will come to rule" and so forth. And that other bit, the "For you will sacrifice the man that clothes me" and yes and so beautiful yes and so true and sounding so much like Himself elsewhere. Okay, and so what if the rest of it is just more noxious bullshit—immortal realm of Barbelo, demiurge Yaldabaoth and Sethian spark, the whole ridiculous celestial bureaucracy and jesus god another luminous cloud. That insufferable self-satisfied laughter so out of character, the evisceration of any meaning in that spiking pain, Christ as only funky guru and salvation as secret frat handshake, pointless mystic knowledge instead of earned through works or faith. Et cetera. But, but, but. And the Church has answered the Gnostics of course, those known long before and Nag Hammadi in '47 and now El Minya, *minha*, mine but back to the point: if Judas was chosen to enable salvation how then was he also chosen for ignominy and pain? The asphyxia as the rope tightens around the trachea, the two or three minutes of struggle, the rippling of muscles along the limbs and abdomen as consciousness is lost, the effusions of urine and feces, the erection and even orgasm, the face now engorged and cyanosed, the petechiae, the protruding tongue as death follows and yes you have researched this and yes and thought and how? And if not hanging, if Acts trumps Matthew, then the headlong fall, the bowels gushing out across the ground. Or both as some now argue or neither as Papias once claimed and in any case in all cases how could that have been permitted much less required? All that happened could have happened without him. To add in his pain and death makes no sense, no sense, no sense.

DIRECTOR: Nobody moves. I'm not kidding. Nobody fucking moves. We have to think this through. Okay, we get some towels, a fucking ton of towels. Some bleach. We get a big plastic bag and a—

LEAD ACTRESS: You're totally and utterly mad. Look at all these people. There's no bloody way we could, even if we wanted to, no bloody way—

DIRECTOR: First of all, Eileen, everybody knows you're not really from England. You're from Indiana, so how about if you fucking talk like it. Second of all, you don't understand, we can't just, he was, look, he was my friend too but there's no way we can just...

LEAD ACTRESS puts on her clothes and leaves the set, followed by OTHER ACTORS AND ACTRESSES, LINE PRODUCER, CAMERA OPERATOR, GAFFER, BOOM OPERATOR, FIRST ASSISTANT DIRECTOR, ELECTRIC INTERN, CINEMATOGRAPHER, SOUND MIXER, HAIR STYLIST, KEY GRIP, FIRST ASSISTANT CAMERA, SET DRESSER, DOLLY GRIP, BEST BOY, MAKEUP ARTIST, PROPERTY MASTER, PRODUCTION COORDINATOR, SCRIPT SUPERVISOR, SET DECORATOR, PRODUCER, STUNT COORDINATOR, UNKNOWN PERSONS. Again the slight hydraulic wheeze as the door closes behind them.

The DIRECTOR stares at the closed door. He wipes his forehead, and walks to where the

> LEAD ACTOR *lies on the floor, blood pooled* *around his head. The* DIRECTOR *starts to cry* *as he caresses the* LEAD ACTOR'S *face.*

DIRECTOR: I'm sorry, man. I'm just so fucking sorry.

They were finally sure, or at least pretty sure. The woman, she had almost definitely been in the crowd that day, had almost certainly still been standing there when the two of them decided to get a cup of coffee. She'd been in the news again last night, just a quick note about the not-guilty plea of the golf-club guy and the woman's upcoming burial. The two young men decided they would go and pay their last respects, because they owed her something, kind of, and besides, how crazy was this whole thing! Turning off televisions for no reason and getting killed for it! They helped each other pick out the right clothes, somber but flattering. They drove to the cemetery and found the grave, and the ceremony was half over by then, but it was even crazier than they'd thought. For one thing, the minister was certifiable, and also drunk. For another, there was hardly anybody else there: the only other mourners were a middle-aged man and two high school kids, a boy and a girl. The three of them had straight-backed chairs pulled right up to the open grave, and they were all crying so hard they could barely sit up straight, so probably family of some kind. The two young men stood off to the side, far enough away so that if they were noticed they could pretend to just be walking by. For a while they listened to the minister and tried to understand what he was saying about Beckett or maybe à Becket? Finally they gave up and just enjoyed the fact of being out in public well dressed with a handsome and gracious and kind significant other; and the warmth and stillness of this late spring morning; and the smell of the grass, the freshly turned earth; and the sight of the hyacinth vines that climbed here and there along the cemetery wall, their lavender flowers and bright purple pods. As the men's gazes moved along the wall they noticed two other burials going on. One was over to the east, and looked as if it was about to end. The other was to the west, just getting started, and the young men watched as a coffin was lifted from a hearse and borne into that distant crowd. They looked at each other, and at the minister, the family, the hole. Then there were shouts, and the young men looked east again, and police were converging on the burial that was nearly done. Its mourners scattered. A policewoman caught up with and tackled one of the fleeing bereaved right there in front of the two young men, and the man's moustache came flying off and landed at their feet. The two young men felt like applauding, and almost did; as the man was handcuffed and lifted and led away, the younger of the two by a month bent down and picked up the moustache. They both looked at it, and the one who'd picked it up put it in his pocket and mouthed, A souvenir! They bit their lips to keep from laughing, and turned back to the drunk minister and whatever he was saying, and now he slurred the final words and it was over. The crying man stood and dropped a rose down into the grave, and the young men heard something like a whisper as it landed. The teenagers stood too, and the boy dropped in another rose, and the girl dropped in a third, and then the three of them held each other, and the minister stared up at the sky and wavered forward over the hole and caught himself just in time. The two young men looked at each other, nodded, turned away. But then instead of heading for their car they took a walk along the cemetery wall, just because it was so beautiful. Halfway along there was a boy trying to catch a lizard, and they stopped to watch. He held a long stalk of field grass, its end looped to form a noose, and he wiped his hands on his tank top, leaned forward carefully and reached out, the noose quivering, the lizard motionless, the noose hovering over it, the lizard springing into the air as the noose tightened around its neck, and then the noose snapped and the lizard shot into a crack in the wall. The boy stared at the crack, at the noose, at the two young men, then screamed Assholes! and vaulted the wall and ran off. The two men laughed unhappily. Again they walked and now stopped again: the crowd at the third burial. One of them turned back but the other grabbed his arm, pointed at a couple who appeared to be bickering. The two young men edged forward and heard the woman say There was no way we could have known, and I'm asking you to please shut up so I can hear what the priest is saying. The man was silent for a moment, then said All I'm saying is there were signs. The thing with the apricot, the thing with the goldfish, the thing with the rings of Saturn. Those were signs, and if we'd just taken the time to— For the last time, shut up, said the woman. The man did. The priest was still talking, sadly and oldly. One of the two young men took the other's elbow and pulled lightly, but the other resisted, shook his head, and so they stayed. The man who had mentioned Saturn now took something from his pocket. It was a tiny package of some sort wrapped in glossy paper the exact same green as the woman's dress. He turned it over and over in his hands until the woman beside him said Will you please, please, please put that goddamn thing away. They're very rare, said the man. And they're not even indigenous to this continent. Mostly Brazil, I think, plus maybe Paraguay. How could— If you go all nutso on me again I swear to God I will beat the living shit out of you right this very minute in front of everyone, said the woman. The man put the package back in his pocket, took it out again and said It deserves a proper burial too. The woman raised her hand and the man flinched. He stared at her for a moment. Then he walked away. The woman hissed at him to come back. The man kept walking. The woman glared, took a step toward him, then turned back to the burial. The man walked right by the two young men, and something happened, the man had the tiny package in his hands and seemed to be putting it in his pocket but it fell to the grass and either he didn't notice or didn't care, and already he was out the near gate. The two young men looked at each other. The older of the two by a month picked the package up, turned it over, shook it. It was very light and didn't make any noise, and he wondered if there was anything inside at all. The wrapping paper was gorgeous up close like this, kind of marbled-looking, less glossy than it had seemed before. He smiled, mouthed A souvenir for me too!, put it in his pocket. The younger man nodded, came closer, leaned his head on his boyfriend's shoulder. He was pretty sure they'd be okay as long as nothing ever ended.

Martin

I. PERSONAL INFORMATION

NAME: Martin

AGE: Mid-to-late 40s

PLACE OF BIRTH: Nazareth, Pennsylvania

BIRTH ORDER: Second of six brothers

DATE OF ADMISSION: 2/18/02

II. PSYCHIATRIC EVALUATION

DATE: 2/19/02

LOCATION: Delta Institute of Mental Health

CONDUCTED BY: Eleanor Riven MD, Ph.D.

III. GENERAL OBSERVATIONS

1. Background
Martin was found lying on the sidewalk just outside the chain-link fence that marks the southern boundary of this facility. In the course of the brief discussion that ensued, it became evident that Martin suffers from the delusion that he is a guitar string. On the authority of this therapist, Martin was coaxed gently inside, in the hope that herein he might receive the treatment he so clearly and desperately needs.

2. Physical Description

Martin is approximately thirty-one (31) inches long and 0.04 inches in diameter; more precise measurements as to his exact length have been postponed until his upper extremity has been sufficiently re-laxed by hypnosis or massage so as to "uncurl." He is apparently both bronze-wound and hand-silked, and at the end of his lower ex-tremity is a small metal ring approximately 0.16 inches in diameter. His touch is unforgettable, and the smell that his body leaves on the tips of one's fingers puts one in mind of subway tokens, old subway tokens, the very same tokens that as a child one might have spread across the floor late on a summer afternoon before one's mother had returned home from work but after one's stepfather had departed subsequent to his surprise lunchtime visit, said tokens deployed in various patterns, at times that of a waterfall, at times that of a rain-bow, at times that of a tornado as seen from above, arabesques spin-ning out and away, etc.

Upon first perusal Martin bears no scars or physical deformities. However, a closer inspection reveals that the upper third of his torso is deformed at intervals of decreasing length, the first and longest of which measures 1.35 inches. The deformations themselves are ap-proximately 0.03 inches long, and take the form of a sort of "flatten-ing" of the corporeal structure; in these places his skin is "shinier" than elsewhere.

Equally subtle are the discolorations that occur between the afore-mentioned deformations. Said discolorations appear to be stains consisting of a mixture of dirt and some sort of light oil, but as Mar-tin's dedication to personal hygiene is otherwise exemplary, particu-larly for someone living "on the street," this seems unlikely.

Unfortunately, Martin is either unwilling or unable to discuss the deformations and discolorations in any detail, other than to say that they are "what's left of the hands what played (him)," which this therapist takes to mean that they are the result of parental, care-taker or conjugal love or abuse as the case may be.

3. Conduct

Martin's delusion is remarkably consistent and cohesive. Taking care neither to condemn nor to collude in his beliefs, this therapist asked him to explain why he believed that he was a guitar string. Instead of answering directly, he insisted that I, this therapist, lodge the aforementioned small metal ring in a wooden notch, wind his upper extremity around a metal peg, stretch him over an ebony bridge, and pluck him firmly. Having of course no such notches, pegs or bridges at hand, and yet seeing no harm in acceding for the moment to his desires insofar as they might be fulfilled within the confines of this facility, I stretched Martin as tightly as possible between the respective backs of two wooden chairs here in our recreation room, securing him in place with the use of large metal clips. I then plucked as requested, a single smooth stroke with my right forefinger.

I was rewarded with our first significant breakthrough, a humming sound, a single prolonged note which, given Martin's coloring and breadth, one might best assume to have been in the key of A. What struck this therapist as of particular interest given its musicological impossibility was the fact that said note appeared to contain the aural characteristics of the minor rather than the major chord in said key. That is, rather than communicating any sort of folk pleasantness, pop mooning or rock aggression, Martin's note spoke instead to certain dark cramped spaces, and did so in a way that made reference not to clichéd midnight trains bound for Georgia or to meeting the devil at the crossroads, but to the at once searing and suffocating sadness that one might experience via, to give a few random examples, the way the light drips from the bare branches of the dogwood in the park across the street as seen from the recreation room's lone window on a February morning; or, a mother's insistence on hiding her gin—foolishly, pointlessly, there was no one from whom to hide it—in the laundry hamper; or, the news of one's stepfather's death at the prison to which one's testimony had unwittingly, unwillingly sent him, etc., at which point I noticed that concurrent with the humming sound, Martin was oscillating furiously. Not wishing to risk a full-blown psychotic outbreak, I unstrung him at once, and thereafter the evaluation continued rather more in accordance with current practice, though occasionally interrupted by Snack Time, Pill Time, Arts and Crafts, etc.

Martin's voice is rough-edged yet mellifluous, and he converses fluidly on all subjects successfully broached. Aside from refusing to respond to certain of my questions on the grounds that the answers were "none of (this therapist's) damn business," he was for the most part polite and cordial throughout our interview.

119

IV. ANTECEDENTS

Repeated attempts were made to determine any and all aggravating and detonating factors, the length of time the patient has suffered from the aforementioned delusion, the number of times he has been hospitalized previously, and the number of times he has attempted suicide. Unfortunately, it would appear that none of this information is any of this therapist's damn business.

V. DIAGNOSTIC APPROXIMATION AND PROGNOSIS

Given the absence of negative symptoms such as affective flattening, alogia or avolition, it is this therapist's opinion that Martin's delusion is more likely psychotic than schizophrenic in nature. He may well respond favorably to pharmaceutical and/or psychotherapeutic treatment, and though of course the duration of said treatment cannot be known in advance, once his delusion is under control Martin will in all probability find himself able to fit as easily into society as anyone else—a society, it should be noted, that hardly deserves the manner in which his baritone hum causes diaphanous sheets of the listener's at once searing and suffocating sadness to float up and away from the listener's body, said diaphanous sheets drifting out the recreation room's lone window, across the street, then catching and tearing and hanging in shreds from the bare branches of that dogwood—in a word, catharsis, etc.

VI. COMMENTARY

Martin presents one of the most interesting cases that this therapist has had the pleasure, though "pleasure" is of course not the word, not exactly, of evaluating in her eighteen years of service here. While it might seem that in Martin's case there is no potential for danger to himself or others, and that outpatient management rather than hospitalization might thus be the most appropriate course of action, particularly given the exceedingly large and ever-growing number of patients with whom he is presently forced to share the recreation room for hours at a time every morning and every evening, hour after hour of their grasping and babble and drool, it is nonetheless this therapist's steadfast position that should Martin be returned to "the street" in his current state, he would undoubtedly eventually, and more probably sooner than later, be relegated to one of contemporary urban society's many many many, if I may, "garbage heaps," the alleys and storm drains and abandoned buildings wherein gather others similarly cast out: the psychotic, the schizophrenic and the simply unbearably searingly suffocatingly sad. If that were to happen, Martin's current state of delusion might metastasize, perhaps to include complications of a depressive nature to a degree that no seratonin reuptake inhibitors could possibly handle effectively, such that he might someday indeed wonder if there is any point at all in even trying anymore, etc., and at that moment may well choose to stretch out on a warm park bench, stare for a time at the sky, close his eyes and slash his wrists. For this reason, though it is well known that involuntary hospitalization may increase distrust, resentment, and the intensity of the patient's delusional beliefs, this therapist must insist that Martin remain at this facility and under the constant care of a trained professional such as myself for as long as his therapist, this therapist, I, me, deems necessary.

Sea Dragon

*O*h bless that man or woman, the one in the lab or factory, the one who first looked up, eyes glazed, forehead sweaty, palms and groin and armpits damp, and smacked his or her sweaty forehead with his or her damp and possibly gritty or chapped or chalk-dusted palm and said, We must make the microwave beep. When it, the microwave, when it is done imparting heat to food or drink, it must beep, discreetly but clearly, and not just once but at regular intervals, for the future eater or drinker may well have been caught up in silver-tipped reveries, may well have forgotten that he or she had ever wished anything heated.

Two minutes ago you traipsed into the laundry room, not ambled or shuffled or waltzed but by god traipsed, and no more stalling, no more fooling around by god it was time. Then you saw the stacks. Good lord, the stacks. The quartz of whites and the mica of darks and the feldspar of delicates all mountained together—it was just too much, just simply way too much for a man in need of java as it was. So out of the laundry room into the kitchen, coffee from pot to mug, mug from hand to microwave, door closed and timer set for sixty seconds.

As the off-center mug began to rotate and revolve you headed from the kitchen into the entryway and out through the front door, you squinted against the hard fat sun and inspected the grass, the grass dying in spots and you knew this, had seen it before and were nonetheless surprised, this dying—but someone could come with gleaming instruments and mysterious substances, could revive the brown grass, could save its very life, the gardener rolling the crash cart up the driveway, running an extension cord from the closest kitchen socket, plugging in the monitor and defibrillator, the electronic squeal confirming asystole, the gardener digging a quick hole and pouring in a quart of epinephrine, he warms up his paddles and at the first hint of flutter shouts Clear! and presses the paddles to the lawn's broad chest, the surge and jolt, the lawn's great heart beating steady once again.

Or else he could cut out the dead part and lay new sod, whichever would be easier.

Back into the house you came, thinking of lawns and heartbeats and your wife at work in her faraway office downtown and your sorry-ass brother-in-law installed in front of the TV upstairs and your infant daughter also upstairs but asleep, or perhaps awake or waking but at any rate silent and you knew this, could be confident of this thanks wholly to the silence of the baby-phone receiver on your belt. You thought of your daughter, the whole of her, you held this in your head but needed more, needed the very thing of her in your eyes; through the entryway and down the hall and up the staircase and only then, from the kitchen, that single beep, discreet, reminding you that your forgotten black bitter coffee was ready to be removed and softened and sweetened, the microwave's microwaves done causing each drop to tremble, and trembling is heat, let us never forget, a certain kind of heat.

And you smiled. Who was that man or woman, that lab-coated or factory-appareled genius? Now, still standing at the top of the staircase, the nearby door to your daughter's bedroom closed, and behind the closed door your daughter asleep or waking or awake and at any rate silent in her crib, its white pillows and their lavender embroidery, your starling-eyed wife dredging spreadsheets for marketing-oriented data in her faraway office downtown, your sorry-ass brother-in-law stretched out and sniggering on the family room floor and beyond him the TV, a game show of some kind and someone has just lost though it's not clear what, the car or vacation or jackpot lost and gone, the host shakes his head, the audience moans, the contestant's shoulders slump, but slowly, the slowest of slumps, and the microwave sings to you again, your coffee ready to be softened and sweetened, back down the stairs and who was that man or woman, the one who dreamt the beep? If he or she were here just now you would pull him or her to your breast, would kiss him or her full on the mouth, better if it were a woman of course, a hairpin-curved wet-lipped et cetera, but even if not, full on the mouth, would then pull slightly back and say to him or her: Thank you. *Thank* you.

Ditto for whoever invented baby-phones.

For without baby-phones you would never have been permitted this time spent not hovering over your daughter's crib, not making sure she was okay, fine, still breathing, this time spent instead heating coffee and observing grass and thinking of surgery and sunlight and your limber-limbed wife making phone calls, important phone calls, to other Sacramento-based marketing-oriented individuals. Down the stairs up the hall into the kitchen and you open the microwave, pull out your coffee (is it steaming? It is!) and take half-and-half from the fridge, stir it in and put the carton away, turn to the cupboard and bring down the bowl and—

And nothing. The sugar bowl is empty. You say a bad word. You open the bin and there is a bag and the bag is empty as well. You say the bad word again, and add a worse one. You remember a photograph taken of you years ago, a high-school ski trip, the photographer your best friend: Jake. And the run, the lift and flex and jump and you in the air (and how far off the ground? Fifteen feet? Twenty-five? Call it twenty though it was probably twenty-five but could have been fifteen) with arms spread wide, one leg stretched out in front and ski-tip to the sky, one leg stretched out behind and ski-tip to the ground (and what was that move called? A dilly? A dally? A doozy?)—the photograph enlarged and so clear that the down-slope pines reflected in your shades, the pines so tinily reflected, those pines could be *counted by the naked eye.*

A daffy!

Yes, a daffy. And if you remember correctly, and you do, it was in fact a double-daffy that you'd pulled, though the photo of course couldn't show the whole move, and just as well that Jake hadn't brought the camcorder along or he'd have got the landing too, the headshot-pheasant landing, the bent-pole snapped-ski bloody-nose landing.

Whatever became of that photo? Of Jake? And why are you thinking of any of this? Ah yes: Sugar Bowl, the name of the ski resort.

Out of the kitchen and down the hall and up the stairs with your coffee soft but still unsweetened. The game show is over; a soap commercial chirps. Your brother-in-law is now asleep, and you walk over and kick him not all that gently in the side.

- Oh, he says. Hey.
- We're out of sugar.
- And?
- And, could you go get some?
- I could, but I'm not going to.
- Les, we—
- Why don't you go get it yourself?
- Because you're the one who pours sugar all over your

cereal and never refills the bowl. Or anything else for that matter. You know what would be cool? If just once you'd—

    - I didn't use sugar this morning. I used honey. The bowl was already empty.

    - ...if just once you'd, well, be that as it may, Les, right now I'm busy, and here it is four o'clock in the afternoon and you're watching game shows instead of out looking for a job, so—

    - You don't look too busy to me. You look to me like you're drinking coffee. Or is that a fundamental part of house-husband-ing? Some kind of essential—

    - Les, could you please just—

    - Yes, I could, and no, I'm not going to.

Which is when you kick him in the face. And then you kick him in the stomach. And then you pour what's left of your soft but unsweetened coffee, the third-of-a-mug or so that hasn't already spilled all over the couch and the carpet and your jeans and the front of your shirt and god*damn*it more laundry to do, you pour that third-of-a-mug straight down his gasping throat and stand back to watch him choke.

Actually, no, that's not what you do, though you imagine it, the whole vivid sequence, you imagine it all in the moment it takes to walk over to where he lies. None of the pouring or watch-ing or choking ever happens because instead of saying I could, but I'm not going to, he stares at you, and you stare at him, and he fi-nally gets up and asks for your car keys, and you tell him to take his own damn car, and he says in that case he needs ten bucks for gas, and you tell him that if instead of going out with his buds every night (and coming home drunk and always always always slamming the goddamn door and waking up the baby that you and your dove-handed wife have just spent two goddamn hours coaxing to sleep, and then when you say Goddamnit Les we just spent two goddamn hours getting her to sleep and now she's awake and we're exhausted and we've both got work in the morning, unlike you, who never does a goddamn thing around this place, never lifts a goddamn finger, he comes right back with some stupid jab about house-hus-bandry versus real work, and you're about to pop him one, about to really just pound some common sense and decency into that stupid-ass skull of his when your wife steps in and tells you to go get the baby and tells him to please try to be more quiet from now on when he comes in, and he nods, brings a stupid drunk finger to his lips, and tiptoes from the room) he'd stay home every once in a while, just stay home and hang out and be normal and maybe watch a movie on cable or something, then maybe he'd have ten bucks of his own to buy his own goddamn gas for once.

No. No no no. None of this happens either, though you imagine it all word for word in the moment it takes for you to set yourself, and to shift your weight, and for your foot to swing forward from its lifted-in-back position and kick him not all that gently in the side. In fact, he never even gets to And? Instead of And? he says Okay, and heads downstairs and you hear the front door open and close, quietly, almost silently, the way you'd close a door if you knew that somewhere in the house a baby was sleeping, and you loved that baby with all your heart. Which is the way he pretty much always closes the door, come to think of it, even when he's just back from hitting the bars with his buds, which only happens, let's be honest, once or twice a month, whereas you, though you, too, love the baby with all your heart, surely more than your brother-in-law does, pretty much by definition more than your brother-in-law ever could, often forget and the door slams behind you and the baby's screams pour through the air and your wife is definitely going to have something to say about it five or ten seconds from now.

So you listen, waiting for an engine to fire up, and you'll know by the pitch of the roar which car it is, yours or his, Hyundai or Ford, but no engine fires, none at all, which is strange, inexplicable, the closest store is six blocks away, and you wonder for a moment, then walk into the baby's room and see that she is in fact still asleep.

Or possibly something much worse.

You set your coffee on the dresser, take a deep breath and do what you must, what you always do when you enter her room as she sleeps, for your fear, your greatest fear of all, greater even than your fears of emphysema and cancer and all other debilitating and/or fatal illnesses especially the ones whose names you don't know or can't pronounce and floods and earthquakes (the big one is coming, you know it is, nothing big this far north since Loma Prieta in '89 and it's been too long and the big one is coming to get you) and wildfires and mudslides and all other natural disasters of any kind, is of course that she has stopped breathing: you watch her chest from across the room. You watch it closely, but not too closely, hoping that this time, for once, the rising and falling of her chest will be easily seen.

And of course it cannot be seen, easily or otherwise.

You count to thirty, forty, forty-two, trying to smack your fear into the corner where it belongs, you know how stupid it is, how very stupid, you swing and swing but it keeps on coming, grows bigger and stronger and worse as if fed by each punch and still no lifting or falling can be seen, easily or at all. So you walk across the room and lean over the crib and again you watch your daughter's chest, hoping that it was just a question of distance, that from here her chest will clearly lift and fall, so that you will not have to do the other thing; still you can't tell if she's breathing and you're just about to do the awful thing but then you remember, color, her color, you check her color and she's yes she's pink appropriate and baby-colored thank you god.

Except.

Except that her breathing could have stopped only seconds ago. At the very moment you were setting your coffee on the dresser she could have stopped breathing and still now be pink though shading towards purple as oxygen-depletion sets in. Is she shading towards purple? It's hard to be sure in this light. So you do it, the awful thing, the thing that brings the other kind of fear, and it's even worse this other kind the kind that surges thick up through your throat—you lean further over the crib, further and further and down and down until your ear is as close as you can get it to her mouth without letting your hair touch her face, for if your hair touches her face however lightly she will wake, will surely wake, will surely scream for hours.

Assuming she's still alive.

You lean. You wait. You hear nothing. You wait again. Nothing. You straighten and gasp. You try again and still nothing, still she is pink, fine, healthy but you can't leave the room until you have heard her breathe: the only acceptable deal. You lower your head yet again and listen and wait, and still no breathing, you wait, and now you hear only everything else, the lawnmower down the street and the flicker rattling the telephone pole, the groan of air-conditioning, your own pulse sharp in your ears and then it happens, she twitches and flinches and your hair must have brushed her face and she's alive! alive! and now she's awake and enraged and opens her mouth to scream; as always your impulse your instinct the first thing you do and how wrong is reach out to cover her mouth and stifle the scream before it starts, you reach and then goddamn!

- Guess not, says Les.

- Big enough, you say. Plenty big enough for me.

- So I see, says your wife. Plenty big enough for you to grab Victoria and get her out of the house but quick. Good thinking, honey. Good work.

She turns to Les.

- And you saved the life of a singing teddy bear.

Les winks at you; you go to speak but he waves you off.

- You should have seen him, he says. You should have seen how he scooped up Victoria and flew downstairs. Flew like a bird, like a nuthatch, exactly like a nuthatch.

- My husband, the valiant nuthatch.

- No, you say. That wasn't it. That's not how it was at all.

Your wife hasn't heard, is now pulling groceries from the car, the back seat and trunk stuffed with bags, and she and Les take a bag in each arm and begin the walk to the kitchen, a laughing joking caravan of bags, and you watch, you hold your daughter and watch, and there will be time to set the record straight, time for all to be clarified, but your daughter is crying, reaching toward the door through which they've disappeared. As your wife calls out asking if you're planning on doing the laundry at some point, you feel your heart grow weedy and ragged and bent, and wonder if it would even be worth the trouble.

Hat

*H*e came in through the door, and they gave him a paperclip and told him to make an airplane. When the airplane is finished, they said, you may go, or you may stay. As you wish.

He took off his hat.

- Am I permitted the use of tools?

Yes, they said. Tools are allowed. Of course, a master would never need them, but the journey is long and you are just beginning. For now, tools are allowed.

- And may I use additional materials?

Of course not. Use what you are given.

❧

With a soldering iron, a file, and two small pairs of needle-nose pliers, in five days he'd made an airplane of the paperclip, and he led them to see it.

No, they said. It is not an airplane.

- But look! The wings, the tail, even the landing gear...

It is not an airplane, they repeated. It is a toy. You must make an airplane.

- What does an airplane have that my toy doesn't?

Your toy has almost nothing that an airplane has, they said. Where is the engine? The propeller? The flaps and rudder, the fuel gauge, the gyro horizon? Your toy is no airplane, sir. Please do not call us again until your airplane is ready.

- Then I will need more tools, and additional materials.

All the tools you like, they said, though a master would never need them. But no additional materials. Use what you are given.

❧

For eight months he labored, epoxy and tweezers, loupe and engraver. Finally the paperclip was an airplane with everything that an airplane must have, and again he led them to see it.

- I have finished, he said. May I go?

No, they said. It is still not an airplane.

- Of course it is. Just look—the oil gauge and altimeter, the removable cowling, the engine with its pistons and valves...

Very well, they said. If it's an airplane, start the engine. Start the engine, fly the plane, and then you may go.

- I have to make it fly?

Of course. Airplanes fly. If yours does not fly, it is not an airplane.

- But— he began. Then he bowed his hatless head, and they walked away.

ༀ

For nine years he labored, centrifuge and compound microscope, laser and interferometer, micro-tomes and -pipettes and -needles. By the time he finished he was blind in one eye, but the airplane was ready, a point of silver-gleaming, wingspan of a millimeter and a millimeter from nose to tail. Then he called for them, and they came. One by one they perused his work. Finally they asked, And does it fly?

- Of course.

With a thread of spider-web he spun the propeller, and the plane slipped along the desktop, lifted and dipped and transcribed Giotto's circle before landing once again on the desktop.

It is a fine plane, they said. You are well on your way.

- May I go?

If you insist. But you are not yet a master. Stay with us, and learn to build without tools.

- One can learn on one's own.

Slowly, said one. Poorly, said another. Those who learn fastest and best are those who learn from those who learned first. Stay, learn from us, become a master.

- No. You have said I may go, and I shall.

So saying, he put on his hat and left.

ༀ

Forty-one years later he returned.

- So at last you have decided to learn more? they asked.

You wish to become a master?

No, he said. I have learned what I wished to learn.

- Is that so? We would accept your word if we accepted the word of anyone. As things stand, we must see proof.

Very well, he said. Bring me a thumbtack, and I will make you a submarine.

- How interesting. And which tools will you be needing?

No tools, he said. Just the thumbtack.

&

The thumbtack was brought, silver-gleaming and sharp. He set it in his hat, and they watched for three days and nights as he taught it to love. On the fourth day he rose, took the thumbtack in his left hand, placed his hat on his head, and led them to the sea. There, he set the thumbtack in the water and taught it to float.

- But it is still just a thumbtack, they said.

Yes, he answered. And no.

So saying, he stepped aboard, took the helm, and submerged.

Follow the Money

With apologies to Elmore Leonard.

Akinfeev watched Xochitl, and she watched him back. He asked if she was hungry or thirsty and she said that she was neither, but that she couldn't wait for the whole thing to be over. He said that soon it would be: Bruyère's bagman would be arriving at the station with the ransom money at eleven o'clock the next morning, and Akinfeev and his private army would be waiting.

Bruyère radioed Trapattoni in the helicopter, asked if the gunboats were on schedule. Trapattoni confirmed that they were. Bruyère asked if the artillery pieces had been successfully emplaced. Trapattoni confirmed that they had. Bruyère asked how many sharpshooters would be up on the roofs. Trapattoni said eight, and Bruyère said perhaps it would be a good idea to add a few more; Trapattoni asked if twelve would be acceptable, and Bruyère said that sounded good to him. He signed off and stepped out onto the veranda where Vlaisavljević was lying on a lounge chair, nursing his beer, eyes closed against the hard low sun. They went over the details of the exchange one last time. Bruyère clapped him on the shoulder, returned to his office, called Ghosh and told her to meet him in the tower at six.

Chichester crept up to the top of the ridge and raised his binoculars. He didn't have anywhere near enough men on the force to stop what was building there at the station. His only hope was that Akinfeev would try to keep both Xochitl and the ransom money, and Bruyère's gunboats and artillery pieces would open fire, and the sharpshooters would do their job, and then maybe, just maybe, he and half a dozen officers on motorcycles could cut through the chaos and get to the suitcase before Trapattoni's chopper hit the ground. And would the serial numbers on the bills be sufficient to get Bruyère put away for money laundering? If not, the bills could always be switched for ones that would do the job. He set down the binoculars, picked up the satphone and patched a call through to Nguyen.

Diefendorf lay flat in the chaparral, waiting for Chichester to scuttle back down off the ridge. He had even fewer men at his disposal than Chichester did, and his only hope was that Bruyère's men would try to keep both Xochitl and the ransom money, and Akinfeev's army would storm the train, chasing whoever had the suitcase out the back side, down the cliff and into the forest. It wouldn't be easy for Trapattoni to track the chase through the dense foliage, and Chichester's moto-cops would be useless when they hit the stand of firs that Diefendorf's men had felled; there was only one route to the cave, and it would be covered. He watched as Chichester slid back from the edge. And would trace amounts on the bills be sufficient to get Bruyère put away for drug trafficking? If not, the bills could always be switched for ones that would do the job. Diefendorf pulled out his walkie-talkie and switched it to the channel he and Kwiatkowski had agreed on.

Eto'o took off her apron and told her boss she was going on break. He grunted, and she slid past him toward the staff room. She had powdered sugar all over her hands and her blouse smelled like grease. She opened a pack of cigarettes, tapped one out. Three more hours and then she could go home. She lit the cigarette, wondered if anyone would be there waiting; I got into bed and stretched out beside my wife, our bodies not quite touching.

Fouhami scratched at the dirt until he found a grub. He took it over to a crevice filled with seepage, rinsed the grub and ate it. He hadn't been out of the cave in almost a year, had no interest in going now, not as long as he could still find food here where Zan would never think to look. He remembered colors and shapes from the bar that night, and other colors, other shapes, light itself, sounds and smells and textures from the whole of that life, and he missed them, but not enough to venture out. He edged to one side, worked his toes to the rim of the hole; he sat down, raked up a handful of pebbles, tossed them in and waited for them to hit bottom. The cave was silent. He waited a moment longer. Still only silence. Smiling, he stood and went to dig for more grubs.

Ghosh nodded to Lapcharoensap at the tower entrance and headed up the stairs as quickly as she could. She arrived out of breath at the top, knocked at the iron door; Bruyère answered, turned without speaking, stepped over an open suitcase and walked to the safe.

Ghosh stood against the far wall as he spun the dial back and forth. When the safe was open she came to stand beside him, took the stacks of bills as he passed them to her, arranged them in the suitcase.

    - So you're really going to pay it.

    - You didn't think I would?

    - I wasn't sure. It's a great deal of money.

    - Yes. But she's worth it. And that's what's bothering me.

    - Sir?

    - She's precisely worth it.

    - I don't follow.

    - If they'd asked for a dollar more, I'd have told them to keep her.

    - They've done their homework.

    - It's more than that. There's something about the ransom note itself.

    - I'm afraid I won't be able to help you there. Have you shown it to anyone else?

    - Vlaisavljević, but he couldn't suss it either.

    - Trapattoni?

    - No sense of smell for things like this—worse than you, even.

    - There is someone else to consider.

    - Who?

    - Joneliunas. She's only fourteen, but she's got a bit of a gift. Shall I send for her?

    - There isn't time.

    - She can be here in an hour.

    - And you trust her?

    - Completely. Akinfeev murdered her mother.

    - All right. I'll finish up here. Have her meet me at the stables.

    - Very well.

    - An hour, Ghosh, and not a minute more.

    - Understood.

Ghosh started down the stairs, turned back, watched Bruyère for a moment—the strength in his hands, his sad calm gaze. Perhaps there was a way.

Hovhannisyan waited at the door to the bunker. When Akinfeev came out, she fell in behind him, asked if her services would be needed this evening. He stopped, turned to look at her, said he thought she'd have appreciated this little vacation she'd had. She didn't reply. He shrugged, said not tonight in any event, though most definitely tomorrow. She nodded. He strode off, and she waited until he had gone, then returned to the bunker door. The guards stared straight ahead. Hovhannisyan had heard that the ransom was four million. She wondered how any woman could come to be worth so much.

I woke up, heard my wife banging around in the kitchen, decided to lie back down for a minute. I'd been dreaming about something big and orange, something awful, not a balloon exactly—something with hair. I heard the stove click on, got out of bed and washed my face, went to my office and organized my notes; there was a chance I'd get it finished today, and if not today then tomorrow. And I thought, Boy, if all this imaginary money were mine, you and I could finally do it. I started working through the places we'd talked about—Florida, Hawaii, Mexico. Then I remembered this brochure I once saw, apartments for sale along the top of some ancient city wall. I don't remember the name of the town, or even what country it was in—Europe somewhere, I guess. Maybe Croatia? It was the most beautiful thing I'd ever seen. The wall was made out of bright white stone, and it rose straight up out of the sea. Offshore there was this little island half-covered with trees. And I thought, me and you up on one of those balconies, a little breeze, maybe some— Then my wife yelled was I planning on taking out the trash at some point or should she just go ahead and have it bronzed. So I took out the trash. She was there in the kitchen, already dressed in her scrubs. She said she'd made eggs but now she wasn't hungry so I should eat them. She pointed at the eggs. They looked pretty good—little sprinkles of something, maybe oregano, all over the top. I said thanks. She said she had a double shift today, but she'd pop back home if things ever slowed down enough. She smiled at me. I said okay. I told her to have a good day, and she kissed me on the cheek, and I watched her go, and I am a sick, stupid motherfucker.

Joneliunas followed Ghosh through the stand of oaks. It was almost too dark to see, but the girl could smell horses, leather, oil. They came out into the open behind the stables, and here the light was soft and whole. Bruyère was waiting. He handed her the note.

She read it twice, handed it back, looked down.

- The woman who wrote this was not afraid.
- Perhaps you need to read it again. She—
- I know what the words say. But she was not afraid.

Ghosh kept her face perfectly still. Bruyère nodded, passed his hand over his eyes.

- That is all you need to know? asked the girl.
- Yes. You may go. And thank you.

He turned to Ghosh.

- So that's that. We'll need to talk through this, but I've got one more thing to arrange first. Meet me in my office in forty-five minutes.

Joneliunas walked back into the trees, then began running. She ran until she reached the far edge, stopped to catch her breath, started running again. Twenty minutes later she was home. She picked up the phone, dialed, waited, spoke:

- Hello, Mom?

Kwiatkowski went over the coordinates once again. So this was it: one last assignment and then he'd make the jump. It wasn't just the difference in salary—he'd also confirmed that the men on Chichester's squad got much better benefits.

Lapcharoensap leaned back against the doorframe. Was it dark enough yet? It was dark enough. All the same, he turned slightly to the side and raised both hands to his face so as to pick his nose in private.

MacMorrow walked down to the station, stood in line, bought his ticket. His trip wasn't until tomorrow, but he wanted to make sure that nothing would go wrong, and you got out of the shower, dried off, put on some jeans and one of those thick linen blouses with the embroidery around the collar, stood in front of the mirror and pulled your hair back into a ponytail, tighter and tighter.

Nguyen went over the coordinates once again. So this was it: one last assignment and then he'd make the jump. It wasn't just the difference in benefits—he'd also confirmed that the men on Diefendorf's squad got paid a much higher salary.

Ogasawara squinted through the dusk at the entrance to the cave.

It was maybe eight feet high but only two or three feet wide. Then he looked across the trail, tried to remember which tree his partner was under, decided it had to be the spruce.

     - Hey, Sýs, he called. Remind me again why we have to spend the whole goddamn night out here.

Papathanasiou checked her nails. They looked fine. Then the telephone rang.

Qadir sent her daughter down through the dark to the well, and asked her son to turn the radio off. The ocean was miles away, but she could still smell it. This year the floods were going to be the worst she had ever experienced. She didn't know how she knew this, but there was no question. And some of them would survive, and some of them wouldn't. She listened as her daughter worked the pump handle, heard the water begin to flow.

Revazishvili asked if it would be all right if she changed the channel. No one answered. She went ahead and changed it to some soap opera, and she remembered having seen that girl's face before, something about an abortion. When the commercials came, Revazishvili looked around. Everyone else in the nursing room lounge was asleep.

Sýs shrugged, and swiped at the clump of pine needles that was obscuring his view of the trail.

     - In case something happens?

Trapattoni spread the map out on the table, traced the route with his finger: the peninsula four miles below the point where the southernmost gunboat would be stationed, the ditch-site, the cove where the skiff was anchored, the border. According to his specs, if he stayed low enough coming off the bluff, no radar would be able to track him once he broke down the coast. All this assuming he could get his hands on the suitcase, of course. Bad odds, but better than none at all.

Úlfarsdóttir got home, changed into her bathing suit and went out to the deck. Her lover was sitting at the edge of the pool, her feet dangling in the water. Úlfarsdóttir sat down alongside her. The sky was starting to cloud up. Her lover began to cry. Úlfarsdóttir reached out, touched the woman's knee. She knew that the crying had nothing to do with the clouds. All the same, in her secret heart of hearts she hoped that she'd someday meet someone who wasn't such a weenie, and I imagined you there at the store, maybe up on a ladder stacking bottles of, whatever, of ginseng and palmetto, ephedra, maybe those big ones of ginkgo biloba my wife is always making fun of even though it really has helped with my asthma. And of course that was right when she called to say there was no way she could make it for lunch, some drunk hit a school bus, most of the kids okay but lots of bruises and scrapes and some cuts from broken glass. I said I was sorry, and she said she was too. I asked what they were doing on a bus in the middle of the day, and she said it was a field trip to the Steinhart. Then I said, Honey, nothing to do with the crash, but I need to know what kind of scars you'd have if you got thrown face-first through a window. There was a little silence. I told her not to worry about it, and she said she had to go but she'd call again when things settled down; I told her I missed her, said it twice, and anyone who doesn't believe I meant it can go fuck themselves.

Vlaisavljević watched as Ghosh picked her way toward the tower. He'd just spoken with Bruyère in the kitchen, and nothing had been said about anyone touching the suitcase until it was time. Ghosh chatted a bit with Lapcharoensap, and he let her pass, but that meant nothing—the man was an idiot. Vlaisavljević waited, then walked over and asked Lapcharoensap what she had said. Lapcharoensap couldn't remember, but it had definitely been official—direct orders from Bruyère. Vlaisavljević nodded, asked Lapcharoensap to contact Bruyère immediately, to have him meet them at the top. He made his way silently up the stairs, and found the iron door ajar. Leaning in, he watched Ghosh open the safe, take out the suitcase, and remove a small amount, perhaps half a million. It didn't make any sense—that wasn't anywhere near enough to risk Bruyère's wrath. Vlaisavljević stepped into the room and cleared his throat. Ghosh spun around, her pistol already in her hand. Vlaisavljević crossed his arms.

- How curious, he said.
- It isn't—
- Of course not. But that just begs the question.
Vlaisavljević watched her eyes and then he knew.
- So. Just enough to make the whole thing go ass-over-teakettle. Akinfeev keeps her or she takes somebody's bullet, and

you—
- Stop. Please stop.
- Okay. But what were you planning on—
- I was going to burn it.
- You know the funny thing? I actually believe you. But of course it can't happen that way.
She stared at him. He shrugged. She turned, replaced the money, put the suitcase away and closed the safe, and he smiled.
- You know, we're not actually so—
Ghosh heard the cough of a silenced pistol, and a dark red flower bloomed in the center of Vlaisavljević's chest. She dove to the side, came up firing. The figure in the door finally slumped. She walked over, lifted Joneliunas' blood-spattered face. The girl died just as Bruyère ran in. Ghosh told him everything, her head dropping when she came to the part about the half-million. Bruyère paced back and forth, waited until she went quiet, turned to face her.
- If you're trying to make me distrust you, it isn't working.
- I—
- Forget it.
He knelt down and closed Vlaisavljević's eyes.
- She got Lapcharoensap too. Slit his throat.
- I take full responsibility, sir. I thought she was—
- Doesn't matter now.
- And how are you going to—
- Zan.
- Are you sure? He's still a bit—
- I know, but he owes me, and he's the only one with the nerves for it.
- Very well.
- And you're going with him.
- Sir, I—
- No arguments. First thing in the morning I'll meet you at the warehouse. For now, clean this mess up, and then go get whatever sleep you can manage.

Wang couldn't make up his mind.

Xochitl slipped the flare gun into her handbag and the pistol into her waistband. Less than an hour to go. She went over Akinfeev's instructions in her head: if everything went well, calmly into the train, remain standing until the suitcase was handed over and its contents were confirmed, take a window seat if possible, and when the train slowed down as it neared its first stop, a bullet in Vlaisavljević's forehead and then out the window, down the cliff and into the forest, wait for dark and pop the flare; if things didn't go well, stay alive by any means necessary until Akinfeev found her. She wiped the sweat off her forehead, and wondered how he would deal with a change in plans.

You put on your make-up, and it took you forever—you're still not very good at it, but you get a little better each time. You put on that pair of heels I bought you, wedged your feet into them knowing they'd give you blisters like they always do and it would be band-aids and old sandals for the next week if not more. You checked your lipstick one last time. You closed your door, locked it, headed straight up the sidewalk without looking to either side. Then at the bus-stop all of the little plastic chairs were broken so you had to stand, and the people passing by in their cars, most of them slowing down to stare at you, they had no idea of course but it felt like they did, and you stared right back at them, and I will always love you for that.

Zan and Ghosh sat side by side, the suitcase on the floor between them. She'd never worked with him before, didn't want to be working with him now. The train neared the penultimate station. Zan shifted slightly in his seat. Ghosh reached down to pull her stockings up, fingered the stun-gun in her ankle holster. Zan scratched at the dark lacework of scars that covered his face. Ghosh straightened and turned to look out the window. The train slowed, then stopped. MacMorrow stood on the platform, holding his wife's hand; he kissed her, said he'd call as soon as he arrived. She told him the kids would be fine, it was only a weekend after all, and he nodded, kissed her again, climbed aboard, smiled at Ghosh and took a seat. The whistle blew and Zan drew his pistol, scattered most of Ghosh's brain across the wall. MacMorrow wet himself, and several other passengers screamed. Zan looked around, picked up the suitcase and stepped to the door, felt a stub of metal pressing into his back. Papathanasiou leaned in close, said she was quite sure this wasn't his stop, pointed him back to his seat. The other passengers had mostly stopped screaming by now, were staring at the floor, at their hands, at the bits of Ghosh's skull imbedded in the wall. Wang finally narrowed it down to vanilla, fudge swirl or red bean. The doors closed and the train began to move. Zan pulled out a handkerchief, daubed at his upper lip. Revazishvili lay in her bed and began to cry, not at any of the soap operas or that made-for-TV movie, stupidest shit she'd ever seen, but for her grandson, the baby born with no arms or legs, her daughter holding the formless infant and saying over and over that everything would be fine. Ogasawara and Sýs sat and waited. Trapattoni radioed Bruyère to say that neither Ghosh nor Zan was responding, that it was not yet clear what had happened. Nguyen and Kwiatkowski observed one another from opposite ends of the platform. Qadir sprinkled cardamom across the top, and the kheer was ready; she closed her eyes, tried to decide whom she would most want to survive, at last chose her son, turned and clawed at the skin of her chest. The train pulled into the final station, and MacMorrow prayed, Zan stood, Papathanasiou took her place behind him, the doors opened, and Akinfeev stared. Hovhannisyan saw the suitcase, knew that the plan had failed and their daughter was most likely dead, fell to one knee. Xochitl hesitated. Vlaisavljević and Joneliunas and Lapcharoensap continued down into the depths of Yama, and Ghosh continued up toward the light of Swarga. Xochitl stepped forward and Akinfeev grabbed at the back of her shirt; she shot him in the face and jumped onto the train, Trapattoni shouted into the radio, the gunboats and artillery pieces and sharpshooters cut loose, Chichester frowned, Diefendorf smiled, half of the private army fell and bled and died and the other half stormed the train as it pulled out, Papathanasiou and Zan returned fire, Xochitl grabbed the suitcase and heaved it through the far window, kissed MacMorrow on the mouth and leapt over him as Zan turned and MacMorrow fainted. Zan and Papathanasiou followed Xochitl out the window, slid down the cliff but she was already well into the trees. Trapattoni radioed Bruyère to say that things had gone bad but he'd follow as close as he could, and Úlfarsdóttir watched as the sky began to lighten; she nudged her lover awake, slid her tongue around the edges of the woman's mouth, anything to make the day start out nice for once. Papathanasiou and Zan knelt and opened fire as Xochitl pulled the suitcase over the last felled fir, she felt one round burn across her scalp and another rip through her left arm, she ducked and dropped the suitcase and fired back. Eto'o sat on her couch, picked up a dirty black bandana and twisted it in her hands. Trapattoni caught glimpses down through the trees, peeled up and away, saw a clearing perhaps five hundred yards ahead and then nothing but forest all the way to the cave; he headed for the clear-ing and it didn't look quite big enough but this was his only chance. Wang figured what the hell, asked for a scoop of each, and the chopper lowered slowly, caught a branch, spun and crumpled and flamed as Nguyen and Kwiatkowski appeared on opposite sides, fired fast and hard and fell, both hit, both begging, now dead. Xo-chitl skirted the crash, found the trail again and followed it but then something was wrong, shapes to either side that didn't quite fit, and she hunched down and waited. You opened the door to the motel room, wondered why I wasn't there yet, closed the shades and plumped the pillows, sat down on the bed and cried just a little as Zan and Papathanasiou surged forward and Sýs and Ogasawara started shooting, Zan killed by Sýs, Sýs killed by Papathanasiou, Papathanasiou killed by Ogasawara, Ogasawara killed by Xochitl, and Bruyère listened for a moment to the staticky hush, then took off the headset and buried his face in his hands. Xochitl limped forward into the cave, deeper and deeper until there was no light; she set down the suitcase and slumped against the cool, smooth wall. Chichester slammed his fist against the door and Diefendorf threw a chair across the room. Fouhami wondered who this was, why she was here, what she'd dragged in; perhaps it was food, and he pounced, buried his teeth in Xochitl's throat, her body flailed and the suitcase teetered, Fouhami reached, caught the handle but the suitcase was too heavy, slipped from his grasp, dropped down the hole and just then my wife got home. It was late, ten-thirty or so, and I was almost finished. I stood up and went to the kitchen, and she was there making a sandwich. I asked if she'd had a hard day, and she said that aside from the thing with the school bus it had actually been pretty good, but there was some blood and something else on her shirt, something kind of greenish-brown, so it couldn't have been all that great. I said there was something I wanted to finish up real quick, and she said in that case she'd go see what was on television, maybe catch up on the news. I went back to my office. A little while later she came in, put half a sandwich on my desk, asked if I wanted a shoulder-rub. I didn't, but I didn't say anything, and she started to rub, and if felt really good. I finally put my hands on her hands, and said thanks but it made it hard to type. She stood there for a second, said okay, she'd head on up to bed, and hopefully I wouldn't be too long. I promised I wouldn't. She kissed the top of my head. I worked for another twenty min-utes or so, still not quite finished but really getting close. I went to the bedroom to make sure she was asleep, and she was, peacefully, one hand curled to her face. I tiptoed to the front door, rolled the car down the driveway and pushed it half a block, got in and started the engine, went two more blocks before turning on my headlights. It started to rain as I passed the Wal-Mart, closed by now of course, big and dark and empty, and the rain was beautiful under the streetlights, and I turned back toward home, then turned around again.

Also by Roy Kesey:

Nothing in the World

Praise for *Nothing in the World:*

"A beautiful, powerful book: mythic, vivid, heart-rending. Kesey reminds us anew of how much power there is in an open heart and the simple declarative sentence. He also reminds us that war is a viral madness, infecting everyone it touches."
—George Saunders, author of *In Persuasion Nation* and five other titles

"Roy Kesey's *Nothing in the World* is as horrific and convincing as a nightmare. At its best it resembles the fever visions of Cormac McCarthy's *Child of God* or Denis Johnson's *Jesus' Son*. In telling the story of one young man caught up in the disintegration of Yugoslavia, Kesey has written a story that pushes us beyond war and strife. Instead, we are taken on a morally shattering forced march to the limits of human endurance itself. It is beautiful, brave, and I will not soon forget it."
—Tom Bissell, author of *The Father of All Things* and two other titles

Nothing in the World is a mesmerizing tale of expulsion and return: this is as much a trance as a story. Here's the Serbo-Croatian War as you've never seen it, its starkness and brutality balanced by the harrowing beauty of its landscapes. Roy Kesey is a fearless and very welcome new writer.
—Anthony Doerr, author of *Four Seasons in Rome* and two other titles

"In haunting, evocative prose, Roy Kesey captures the horrors of war, the insanity of genocide, as well as the fleeting joys of love. *Nothing in the World* is a memorable debut."
—Laila Lalami, author of *Hope and Other Dangerous Pursuits*

"Roy Kesey is a natural story-teller, like the other Kesey, but writes about a wider world. This journey from an idyllic Croatian island life into the landscape of war is reminiscent of Cormac McCarthy's *Blood Meridian*—everything is taken away, and all that is terrifying is beautiful—but Kesey's writing also has the moral and figurative power of fairly tale. *Nothing In The World* will surprise you by how big it is."
—David Vann, author of *A Mile Down*

Acknowledgements

For a great many different sorts of assistance, my deepest thanks go to: Eric Abrahamsen, Claudia Frías Amat y León, Bob Arter, Stephany Aulenback, Aaron Burch, Steven Chiu, Pia Ehrhardt, Elizabeth Ellen, David Gerard Fromm, Alicia Gifford, Mary Gillis, Steve Gillis, Sue Henderson, Erin King, John Leary, Pasha Malla, Jim Morris, Roger Norman Morris, Jim Ruland, Steven Seighman, Seth Shafer, Keith Taylor, John Warner and Dan Wickett.